PRAISE FOR YELENA MOSKOVICH'S *VIRTUOSO*

"A hint of Lynch, a touch of Ferrante, the cruel absurdity of Antonin Artaud, the fierce candour of Anaïs Nin, the stylish languor of a Lana del Rey song... Moskovich writes sentences that lilt and slink, her plots developing as a slow seduction and then clouding like a smoke-filled room."
—**SHAHIDHA BARI, *THE GUARDIAN***

"A bold feminist novel: it contains a world of love and friendship between women in which men and boys are both indistinct and irrelevant... *The Natashas* was a fascinating debut, *Virtuoso* is even better... It is the *Blue Velvet* to her *Eraserhead*: a fully realized vision of a strange world."
—**KATHARINE COLDIRON, *TIMES LITERARY SUPPLEMENT***

"If Ferrante's *Neapolitan* series was condensed into one book and that one book was turned into a person who spent a good deal of time at queer punk shows on X, but then they got clean and a job where they wore pumps and a pencil skirt and longed for all the selves they had to abandon to survive—and then that person became a book—this would be that book."
—**GALA MUKOMOLOVA, *NYLON***

"*Virtuoso* is a fine, fraught, strange novel... it will be fascinating to see what she writes next." —**ALEX PRESTON, *THE GUARDIAN***

"*Virtuoso* didn't simply engage me on an intellectual level, but also on a deep and emotional one... goddamn impressive."
—**JOSEPH EDWIN HAEGER, *THE BIG SMOKE***

"The prose poem-esque vignettes that make up the novel *Virtuoso* are propulsive and exact and Yelena Moskovich's language oozes with sensory experience... *Virtuoso* is a queer and transnational novel that hypnotically dunks the reader into every scene." —NATE MCNAMARA, *LIT HUB*

"*Virtuoso* is powerfully mysterious and deeply insightful, a page-turner precisely because you have no idea what to expect. In the era of #MeToo, Moskovich's arrestingly close and complicated view of lesbian relationships and female friendship seems more urgent than ever before. But it's perhaps the novel's defiantly surrealist style that is its greatest triumph."
—NADIA BEARD, *LOS ANGELES REVIEW OF BOOKS*

"This tightly woven feminist novel is a deep exploration of womanhood spanning decades, continents, and digital spaces... *Virtuoso* is a moving book that defies categorization."
—WENDY J. FOX, *BUZZFEED*

"[*Virtuoso*'s] prose is lyrical." —JUNE SAWYERS, *BOOKLIST*

"*Virtuoso* is a novel / is a performance / is a dance with movements and variations / is poetry / is film / is a palette splattered with colors / is a body out of breath. *Virtuoso* is truly a sensual euphoria, one that must be experienced firsthand."
—CAMERON FINCH, *MICHIGAN QUARTERLY REVIEW*

"Haunted and haunting... Told through multiple unique, compelling voices, the book's time and action are layered, with possibilities and paths forming rhythmic, syncopated interludes that emphasize that history is now."
—LETITIA MONTGOMERY-RODGERS, *FOREWORD*, STARRED

"A Best Small Press Book from 2020"
—**MALLORY SMART,** *MAUDLIN HOUSE*

"Moskovich breaks almost every rule of contemporary fiction."
—*KIRKUS*

"[*Virtuoso*] tells the stories of four queer European women in a filmic, fragmented style… An unexpected reunion ties together all the stories in an emotionally complex and gratifying ending."
—*PUBLISHERS WEEKLY*

"Moskovich dwells with indigenous belonging and a native fluency in the realms of the unseen, the worlds slotted between worlds, or behind them, a fluttering geography of veils calling for mirrors, or perhaps for the abolition of mirrors."
—**JOHN BISCELLO,** *RIOT MATERIAL MAGAZINE*

"*Virtuoso* jumps through time involving three pairs of sapphic women, ranging from childhood friends, marriage, and scandal. The paths of these women sync and blend together like waves, written in an almost abstract form. These are loves intertwined with melancholy and mystery."
—**ANDREW KING, UNIVERSITY BOOKSTORE (SEATTLE)**

"With incredible characters and sharp narration, *Virtuoso* illustrates the many ways in which women don't follow the stereotypes created for them."
—**JAYLYNN KORRELL,** *INDEPENDENT BOOK REVIEW*

"Moskovich's novel spills-over with the nuances of existence (and by extension, co-existence), grounding readers in her dizzying and dreamlike story of love, friendship, and reconnection."
—**KAITLYN YATES,** *THE ARKANSAS INTERNATIONAL*

"Moskovich writes with the eye of a film director and the lyricism of a poet."
—MALLORY MILLER, *PAPERBACK PARIS*

"The author's inimitable style is both elegant and poetic. By story's end, our characters' lives amazingly, but not unbelievably, intertwine, skillfully arranged by Moskovich."
—VIRGINIA PAROBEK, *WORLD LITERATURE TODAY*

"*Virtuoso* is a striking probe into feminine love and friendships, an examination of the dichotomy between the individual and the bleeding of self into other which occurs in relationships."
—BETH MOWBRAY, *NERD DAILY*

"Moskovich's dreamlike prose and fragmentation make the introduction of the surreal feel natural in the world she has painted for us." —HAYLEY NEILING, *HEAVY FEATHER REVIEW*

"*Virtuoso* is novel in the most original sense… In Moskovich's inspired hands, language becomes a fragile and shifting musculature, a substance both firm and ephemeral, simultaneously the stuff of our lives and the stuff of dreams."
—ALEXANDRA KLEEMAN, AUTHOR OF
YOU TOO CAN HAVE A BODY LIKE MINE

"Part Ferrante, part Despentes, Yelena Moskovich is a brutal but tender-hearted chronicler of women in love."
—BARBARA BROWNING, AUTHOR OF *THE GIFT*,
I'M TRYING TO REACH YOU, THE CORRESPONDENCE ARTIST

Praise for Yelena Moskovich's *The Natashas*

"Strange and carnal; a riddle of language, the body, and the artistic impulse." —*Kirkus Reviews*

"Dreamy and impressionistic, Moskovich's novel deftly illustrates the many ways women are commodified and objectified by society in both macro and micro ways."
—**Kristine Huntley**, *Booklist*

"The text stacks its scenes like building blocks, creating a mosaic of surrealist serendipity in which everything you think you know dissolves, again and again… *The Natashas* presents a Murakami-esque pictogram of incomplete data that will mesmerize the reader long after the last page has been turned."
—**Samantha Kirby**, *The Arkansas Review*

"*The Natashas* is beautiful, original and distinctive—a stunning new voice." —**Jenni Fagan, author of** *The Panopticon*

"From the surrealistic imagery written with inimitable flair, to the biting grit of the story's exploration of sexual objectification and self, *The Natashas* is utterly captivating. Lyrical, brooding, and delightfully dreamlike, the novel is a strange and ruthless journey into the ailing heart of humanity — and a bizarre peek into the mind of a brilliant new novelist."
—**Michael A. Ferro,** *Michigan Quarterly Review*

"Closest in tone and plot to a David Lynch film… confounding and beguiling in equal measure; prose that reads as heady yet ephemeral as smoke."
—**Lucy Scholes,** *The Independent*

"Wonderfully original... if you are a fan of David Lynch or Haruki Murakami, this sort of joyful acceptance of the bizarre will come easily... Moskovich's debut offers something different, and sometimes we all need that."
—**KIRSTY LOGAN, *THE GUARDIAN***

"Brave, original... written in a Cubist jumble of voices, languages, and textures, *The Natashas* reads as if one were spinning a radio dial of the world... Moskovich's prose radiates with heat as she describes the life animating the city from within, a breath that unites us in our humanity, even the most marginalized— those whose identities are subsumed into the categories of their catastrophes: hostages, refugees, slaves. In *The Natashas*, Moskovich locates that delicate point of equilibrium between aesthetics and outrage."
—**LAUREN ELKIN, *FINANCIAL TIMES***

"Conceptually challenging and aesthetically inventive... Moskovich's narrative voice has the quality of floating slightly above its characters, evoking the disconnect, not only between mind and body, but between individuals, between action and intent, thought and speech.."
—**ELEANORE WIDGER, DUNDEE UNIVERSITY REVIEW OF THE ARTS**

"A haunting, unknowable novel, and no less beguiling for that."
—**ELENA SEYMENLIYSKA, *THE TELEGRAPH***

"As mysterious as a David Lynch film, *The Natashas* paints a dark, post-modern picture of loss of identity, invisibility and disconnection."
—***THE TIMES LITERARY SUPPLEMENT***

"A hallucinatory torrent of imagery and ideas that moves entirely according to its own rules… Moskovich explores the relationship between our identities and our physical selves in an experimental, fragmented narrative, obstinately refusing to reach an orthodox resolution but nevertheless casting a beguiling spell that beckons deeper into its strangeness."
—**ALASTAIR MABBOTT, *THE HERALD SCOTLAND***

"A dark literary novel… an intense Lynchian atmosphere."
—***DIVA***

"Explorations of sexual power, force and identity underpin this beautifully written dreamscape debut by Yelena Moskovitch… a novel that slips and slides through space and time, unmoored by linear convention."
—***ECLECTIC***

"A sulphurous and enigmatic novel, fascinating and astounding… We await the sequel with impatience."
—**FRANÇOIS BUSNEL, *LA GRANDE LIBRAIRIE (FRANCE 5)***

"*The Natashas* is a novel of tact and image, obsessively moving between dry and wet, powder and brilliant. Cosmetics return to its literal meaning: it organizes the world, the cosmos—here according to the masculine desire, both totalitarian and violent."
—**ERIC LORET, *LE MONDE***

"With the eccentricity that her characters assume and the freedom her fiction seizes, Yelena Moskovich, born in Ukraine, who lives in France and writes in English, lands on the literary scene like a Sputnik with extraordinary talent."
—HÉLÉNA VILLOVITCH, *ELLE FRANCE*

"The text is worthy for its carnal and atmospheric writing, which captivates like poetry in prose."
—DAVID CAVIGLIOLI, *L'OBS*

"We open this book like opening a bottle of perfume. It is intoxicating, then hypnotic, and finally completely destabilizing… We emerge from this story a bit shaken, as if after a bad dream. And yet curiously, we want to go back…"
—RÉMI BONNET, *LE POPULAIRE DU CENTRE*

"A brilliant, whirling text, raw and full of imagery, written in a breath both realistic and magical—magnificient!"
—*AXELLE MAGAZINE*

"A sulphurous novel with a disturbing and dreamlike intrigue, a lynchian atmosphere."
—SEAN J. ROSE, *LIVRES HEBDO*

A DOOR BEHIND A DOOR

A NOVEL

YELENA MOSKOVICH

Two Dollar Radio
Books too loud to ignore

Two Dollar Radio
Books too loud to Ignore

WHO WE ARE TWO DOLLAR RADIO is a family-run outfit dedicated to reaffirming the cultural and artistic spirit of the publishing industry. We aim to do this by presenting bold works of literary merit, each book, individually and collectively, providing a sonic progression that we believe to be too loud to ignore.

TwoDollarRadio.com

Proudly based in
Columbus
OHIO

🐦 @TwoDollarRadio

📷 @TwoDollarRadio

f /TwoDollarRadio

Love the
PLANET?
So do we.

Printed on Rolland Enviro.
This paper contains 100% post-consumer fiber, is manufactured using renewable energy - Biogas and processed chlorine free.

♻ 100%   **PCF**   BIO GAS ENERGY   ∞ PERMANENT

Printed in Canada

SOME RECOMMENDED LOCATIONS FOR READING *A DOOR BEHIND A DOOR*: In a doorway. On your way out. Out of your body. In someone else's body. In full honesty. While petting a dog. While losing faith. While finding your keys. As you are, where you are, how you are, finally. Or pretty much anywhere because books are portable and the perfect technology!

AUTHOR PHOTO⇢ Courtesy of the author

COVER ART⇢ Yelena Moskovich, *Facing myself,* autoportrait, 2015

"Be bad, but at least don't be a liar."

Leo Tolstoy, *Anna Karenina*

"Yes, my angel," she says, without looking at me.

Guillermo Rosales, *The Halfway House*

A DOOR
BEHIND
A DOOR

MY ANGEL

NICKY

Nicky, Nicky, Nikolai.

FLOOR SIX

I was a fat baby. I was lying in my crib like an egg yolk. The old lady was upstairs on floor six. Her dining room, above our bedroom. She dropped to the floor and made our ceiling lamp sway, Oh no, Oh no.

OH NO

There was a punctured scream. It wheezed. It lacked its high notes. It fell out of her mouth like a dog's tongue.

THE BOY

His footsteps were as soft as rain—and scared, and stupored—down the stairs.

GOODBYE

She was left to lie there. Three wounds. Her head flopped against her forearm, leaking.

FLOOR FIVE

Nikolai Neschastlivyi lived on floor five, like us. He was much older than me, but also far from adulthood. Mulling, teenaged. He must have had a groin filling with pubic hair. A mother with eyes that could mourn raspberries. No father. And the street dog that he was supposed to leave alone. Vaska. He snuck him in and gave him meat-bones and let him sleep under his bed every now and then.

LISTEN
Like us, they were nothing special.

EVERYONE KNEW
But the old lady, she was different. She was *good*.

I'M SORRY
I can't say her name. I'm afraid it'd call her back from the dead. No one who left this world unjustly comes back with a clear head.

LET'S JUST CALL HER THE OLD LADY, OKAY?
Misery had already come to her. She wore the black veil for her one and only son who drowned in Odessa at age ten. Her husband had just passed a couple years before—an immune system anomaly. They say men leave. They say women mourn. She lived our proverbs.

BUT YOU KNOW WHAT?
She didn't grow bitter. She didn't become hard. She continued to look fondly at children. Because all children were innocent in her eyes. Even the child who accidently horse-played her son to death that August years ago. Even the one who would grow up to be the poor soul to stab her thrice. Nicky, Nicky.

SOFTNESS
How long must we carry it as affliction?

SPEAK UP
Nicky was fourteen when I was just over a year old. I watched him from my mother's arms with my globular brown eyes. He was cuffed. He was smacked around by the *militzioner*, the cop. His mama ran down the stairs, crying.

MAMA'S TEARS
He's just a boy, he's just a boy! But boys don't stab old women once, twice, thrice. That, my *dorogaya mamasha*, is intentional manslaughter, the cop said. But he didn't mean it, she's crying, of course he didn't mean to, just ask him, she's spreading her fingers wide into the officer's face, it was an accident! The cop turns to the boy. He pushes him against the railing. He says, Speak up, *malchik*. Did you mean it?

BAD BOY
Nicky was a bad boy and he went to prison to become a bad man.

YEARS PASSED
I forgot all about Nikolai from floor five.

AND THE OLD LADY WHO GOT STABBED?
What was her life, lived with such precise values, against ours, unfolding into daylight like a corn being husked.

AMERICA
I grew like a cat being picked up by its skin. I stretched out my

baby-chub into loose limbs and a curved stare. My intellect went vertically. Deep and high. On the lateral level, I suppose it didn't always show. We were part of that Soviet diaspora of '91. Our immigration papers got approved. We settled into Milwaukee, Wisconsin.

THAT'S WHAT HAPPENED

I got a so-so education. I finished high school with colorless competence. I had flashes of spirit, but mostly doubt, mostly apathy, and so I got to working.

The plan was to save up a bit, then go to college. I could think about what it was I'd study in college as I was saving up a bit.

BUT THE THING IS

The longer I worked, the more intention scared me. And then I fell in love with an angel.

FEVER

Angelina, an American girl. Half Puerto Rican. Pale and dark at the same time. Her brother called her The Flu when she was little.

Her brother, like mine, elsewhere...

BECAUSE IT WAS DESTINY

I met her at the lesbian bar on the East Side. She was one of the girls attending college at UW-Milwaukee. I just had my GED. And my left-foot kind of charm. She was studying to be a nurse. I circled her. I glared and gawked. She had her heavy, dark hair behind one ear. One lobe showing, smooth and earnest, pierced with a large gold hoop. She turned around. Her eyes ran liquid down my throat. She is my angel. I told her so. She didn't ridicule me. She could have. But she didn't. She welcomed me as pure and sound.

DESTINY CONTINUED

It was easy between us. Our glances laced up. Because it was meant to be. Because the only thing that makes this body bearable is that we can get out of it.

SO HERE I AM

Living with my Angelina. We share a sixth floor apartment with a small balcony. I'm taking some extra courses, getting my administrative skills up. Otherwise, it's temp work. Inventory stock in warehouses. I like counting. Some secretarial jobs. Johnson Controls near the Bayshore Mall. The pharmaceuticals company off the highway. The red-brick building with a small parking lot impossible to turn into from the main road. Filing and copying and answering the phone. I play a game where I ricochet off every request.

THE WORST, ACTUALLY

It's when there are no jobs at all. Every day is like a wounded bird cupped in the palms of Angelina.

THE CALL

Almost midnight. Angelina is already asleep when my phone begins buzzing on the nightstand. I reach over and the screen displays a number without a name. I hold the shaking phone. I put my feet on the carpet and put my weight on them discreetly. I hurry with muted steps into the hallway so I don't wake up Angelina. There, I touch my phone.

"*Privet.*"

No one calls me speaking Russian except my parents. And my parents don't call me anymore.

"It's Nicky. It's Nikolai."

I'm trying to place his tone.

"Nicky? Nikolai?"

"From floor five…"

That old apartment in the Soviet Union. The sound of creaking. The wooden stairwell. Someone running. The lamp, the lump, the lock.

"I'm in America now," he says.

"In America…"

"I've been traveling. I'm near you, Olga."

"And where am I then?" I call his bluff.

"Off Teutonia Avenue."

I don't say anything.

"On the north side. I'm on the south side," he continues.

"That's a bad area," I say.

"I'm a bad man," he replies.

HELL

Nikolai's voice takes a dip. He's murmuring. He's got a dripping faucet from his childhood that keeps wetting his syllables.

"How the hell did you get my number," I whisper.

He's thinking about it.

"Sunrise, sunset…"

He's thinking about it.

"It was mathematics."

He's thinking about it.

"I'm a lone sailboat, I've always been…"

"You stabbed an innocent old lady, Nicky," I interject.

"I'm paying my dues."

His throat cracks. He pauses, to swallow.

"I'm going to Hell, Olga."

"Well, what are you doing in America then?" I ask.

"To get to Hell," he says in a low voice, "they take you through America. There is a door behind a door."

NONE OF MY BUSINESS

It's not my place and it's none of my business. But sometimes you can feel it when a person has the same twist in their heart as you.

MEMORIES

Back then. Most of our other neighbors were either drunks or hags or sulkers or government tattlers or thieves or con artists or too tired to be nice. She was alone. She was patient. She was soft. The old lady. Rest her soul.

I HATE HOW MEMORY FEELS ON ME

There's Time and there's Death and there's a succession of lies trying to braid my hair.

CORRECTION

There's also love. I mean, the yearning for. It is enough to civilize a child. A caress without weight. A rule to follow.

NOW I'M GROWN AND HE'S GROWN

And it's the body that's difficult.

THE DIFFERENCE

Unlike Nicky, who's been who-knows-where all this time, I am an American citizen. I have a good American accent (though I still can't pronounce the word "thief," zief, fiev—forget it).

Unlike Nicky, who probably hasn't had any kind of loving since they took him away to prison, I have a girlfriend. We love each other very deeply and also daily and also toward the horizon.

Unlike Nicky, who sounds like he's pretty much damned, I have fallen in love with an angel and now I know that I am a pure and loveable soul.

JUST ONE THING

Long after the old lady was stabbed, we all felt sorry for Nicky's mama. What a curse, to have a son who'd stab an old lady—and for what? He didn't even take anything from her in the end. For what? Because of his soul. Because his soul was a stabbing kind and it was so strong within him, that it couldn't even wait for adulthood to stab, it flung out from the teenage boy.

OH NO

"I'm a bad man," Nicky says.

OF COURSE

The line went dead right after that.

FORGET IT

I plug my phone back into the charger and put it on the night-stand at my side of the bed. I slide as quietly as I can back under the covers near Angelina's warm, peaceful body. I tell myself, just like that damned word you can never pronounce, forget it. Forget Nicky, Nicky, Nikolai from floor five.

DREAMS

They are blocks of nothing. Dreams, heavy and blank. They pile upon me like weighted blankets. I can hear myself in my dream saying, Wake up. But the dreams hold me inside.

MORNING

When I wake up, Angelina is already at work. Then it's almost noontime. I have no work. I have cereal and coffee. I look online for job opportunities. I go to the couch. I hook my chin over the back cushion and look through the window at the sidewalk far below.

Angelina, who's at the clinic now. Angelina, soft and assuring. Probably filling out a form, or swabbing a bit of skin. All with her creamy, dark eyes.

IDLENESS

I pick up what I can of me. I go to the bedroom. I get in our bed. I masturbate to the color of her eyes.

BAD THINGS

I've never killed anyone. Not even in dreams. Not even in daydreams. Not even in the afternoons when I'm sitting between jobs, looking from the window at the pavement with a fierce void.

I've never stabbed anyone. Not even poked. Not even with the handle. Or the dull edge.

I've never hit anyone. Not even with the palm. Not even with a fist. Or a leg. Or a convenient kitchen object, like a pan. Or a convenient living room object, like a book. Or a convenient bathroom object, like the plunger.

Not even with an unexpected item, like a loose brick from a to-be-repaired chimney (like Miss Anya from floor one did to her husband one night when he was asleep in bed. We heard his snoring, then a flap of voice—part man, part fish. We all listened with our lights off. The ambulance came. Some folks from floor three took bets. He didn't die.).

Not even with a quick-on-your-feet home goods concoction like a pillowcase full of silverware (though I prepared one for an occasion, but then got sucker punched and can't remember why I didn't strike first, I had planned to, I faltered, but that's another story).

BUT NICKOLAI
He has done one of those things and he'd done it once, twice, thrice.

DON'T ASK
How do we know that the soul is good when the mind is filled with foul things?

A NUMBER WITH NO NAME
My phone is ringing in the living room where I left it next to my computer with my CV file open and my internet tabs of classifieds and the cold pool of sweet milk at the bottom of my cereal bowl.

"*Privet*," he says.

HIS VOICE IS DAMP
I'm not sure if it's meant to be threatening. It's not.

"Listen, just listen," he's insisting.

"You shouldn't have called back," I say firmly. "You shouldn't have called at all."

"Don't hang up, Olga."

"Maybe I will."

"Stop—"

"What's this got to do with me?" I insist.

"Believe me, it's got to do with you," he says with a sudden emptiness.

"Okay, listen, Nicky, I don't know how you got out, or got to America, or got my number, but if you're looking for my money, I don't got any of that, so it's *bespolezno*, no use, got it?"

"I'm not looking for money."

"Well what are you looking for?"

There's a crack on the line.

BE CAREFUL

When Angelina comes home from work, I'm on the gray metal slab of a balcony we got off our apartment, smoking. The sliding door is open.

Her purse is on the couch and she wants to kiss me, Hello.

I turn around and arch my back over the balcony railing. My cigarette is between my fingertips. I'm blowing smoke up into the dark sky.

"Be careful," she says, reaching out to me.

NOTHING TO TELL

I don't mention the phone calls to Angelina. They are part of the old world. My life, split in two. Nicky knows. But what good is it, to know?

THE OLD WORLD

It's not just a place and time.

SLAPSTICK

A Soviet childhood in the West.

ALL IMMIGRANTS ARE CHARLIE CHAPLIN
He had eyes like the old lady, by the way. Tragic, ritualized mother.

I NEVER TOLD ANGELINA ABOUT NICKY
Because I never told her about the murder in our building, because I never told her about the feeling of anachronistic dread.

IT'S DIFFERENT THAN HIDING
I told her we had odd neighbors. I told her that my little brother, Misha, was handsome and sickly long before he took off. I told her that my parents were different than her own, because they were ghosts of an era—anxious, angry, unable.

IT'S DIFFERENT THAN A SECRET
It is airborne and obvious. It is in my posture. It is in my gloomy charisma. It is in the way I pick up cues.

IT'S A LAPSE IN LANGUAGE
An air bubble between two continents.

BESIDES LIFE DID NOT STOP
After the old lady was murdered. There were daily worries to tend to. There was my father's shaky position at the agricultural engineering plant. And my mother's intellectual affair with her colleague. And then my baby brother Misha was born with weak lungs. And Miss Anya from floor one accused my mother of trying to seduce her husband (before she almost killed him herself with the stray brick). My mother had to explain that she wanted nothing to do with that first-floor grunt of a man in a polite and convincing manner. Still there were those who sided with

Miss Anya. My mother was Jewish and beautiful and couldn't be trusted. My father was Georgian and stubborn. I had my mother's looks and my father's character. My little brother Misha had ghostly eyes and took long, winded breaths. I tried to look after him.

MISHA AT EIGHTEEN

I won't get into the details, but at eighteen, Misha had only one functioning eye. Otherwise he was perfectly healthy. A miracle— I mean, his lungs.

But he was far away. He stopped talking to me. Then he skedaddled from our home altogether. Didn't tell us where. Said don't call. Don't try. Said leave me alone. I didn't know what to do. I was busy being a deadbeat myself. I was twenty and living at home. This was before Angelina. Before that kind of faith. I guess I could have figured it out. His whereabouts. I heard he was somewhere on the East Side. On what money, I don't know. I guess I could have tried to find him. To tell him, Come back. Come home. But who was I to talk? Who was I, to open my palms and show him my handful of community college credits going nowhere. I don't know if it was an excuse. I believed it at the time. I thought, He's better off out there, in the American glimmer of happenstance, than with us.

DINNER

Angelina is setting up the dinner table. Rice with chicken and peas. I love peas. My angel knows that. I come in from my cigarette. We sit down and start eating.

I'm awfully quiet, I know.

SPEAKING OF GOD
So Misha got Jewish. Heard he prays now. Heard he believes in God. Heard he goes by Moshe.

FOR THE RECORD
I never said God was bullshit.

Maybe I said it once.

I said it because I heard our Babushka saying it back in the day. *God is bullshit.* It sounded right. I personally have nothing against God. Babushka had a lot of pain. It was God's fault. I don't have any pain. Just a sense for suffering. I think it's in my nature. I don't blame God. I think the Almighty gave me a decent life. Not the Lord's fault I am ungrateful.

DESSERT
I often tell myself, Olga, you've got an angel who loves you back and you're acting spooky. The ungrateful shall not be blessed.

BACK IN OUR BEDROOM
I feel more like myself. I'm not in my words. I'm in my T-shirt and underwear. I take off the T-shirt. I take off the underwear. I'm naked. You don't need words when you're naked.

Angelina's wearing her pajama shorts and camisole, satiny like her voice.

Satiny, satiny, her thigh and her shoulder.

She glances down at me, curled around her knees. She knows what I want. She smiles with the knowledge. What I want. I want. She leans over me and lowers down, down. I'm arching my face up, up. Then we are kissing. Just the lips. Just touching lips. Light kisses.

DOVES
First we kiss like doves above the flood.

EARTH, LAND, HOME
We slide our tongues into each other's mouths.

WHAT I WANT
I want. To swallow her tongue.

I WANT
What I want. To fill up her mouth.

DOWN, DOWN
To pour my own long, heavy breath down her throat.

UP, UP
The tips of her hair, the tips of her fingernails, the tips of her nipples.

OUR HEAT CONVERGING
It's a miracle that we are both so wet and alive.

SLEEP
It's the third-degree of night. My eyes open. My phone is buzzing on my nightstand. I grab it and paw my way out of the bedroom so I don't wake up Angelina.

"Enough is enough," I whisper into the phone.

"It's urgent," he huffs.

I find my pack of cigarettes and my lighter. "What is it?"

I throw my long blue coat over myself and quietly pull open

the glass door to step out onto the balcony. It's dark and watery outside. My skin prickles and my shoulders shiver involuntarily. It feels good to be naked in my slouchy blue tent of a coat, my bare heels on the cold slab of concrete.

"You've got to come meet me," Nicky says.

"I don't have to do anything you say," I tell him.

"Listen, Olga, listen to me…"

I'm leaning on my elbows upon the railing like a dog on guard, smoking in slow drags.

"I'm listening…"

"They've got your brother."

"My brother?"

"Moshe. Moshe… Isn't that your brother?"

LOVE

My lit cigarette is falling six stories into the night.

"Olga… Olga…?"

My two empty fingers, my two dumb-struck fingers.

"Please… please… don't hang up."

I don't know how to love people who aren't there.

THERE IS AN HOUR

When the traffic lights switch to blinking yellow. There is an hour when sleep becomes a waking thing.

I've got my pants on, they're slack and dark and ample. And my loose woven sweater. And my long blue coat with deep pockets. Luckily, Angelina is a deep sleeper.

"The diner on 79th and Capitol."

At the door, I put on some lipstick. It gives my mouth some weight.

I've taken her car keys and I'm shifting my way through the stairwell to the apartment garage.

THE HIGHWAY IS EMPTY

The signs pass. The white lines. The yellow lines. My headlights cross and merge ahead. The air falls out of my nostrils onto my top lip. Brother. Sister.

79TH AND CAPITOL

I turn into the parking lot. Low lit, gummy. A couple cars parked in the shadow of the lamplight, probably just the staff. I lock Angelina's dark blue sedan and make my way to the entrance door. Her car is the exact color of the night. When I look back, it almost disappears. Vacant, recessed, no use. This hour plays tricks on the thing that's behind the mind. I walk forward where forward should be.

THE ENTRANCE

It's not a twisted banner. There, near the doors. It's a man.

He unfolds. He's much bigger now. Unbuttoned Soviet leather jacket, scuffed lapel, cracked leather, dangling threads. It sits on his shoulders like a box. Underneath, it's just a faded work shirt, stiff white cotton with thin gray stripes. His gray trousers puff and cave. His face is covered by his Milwaukee Brewers baseball cap.

He's somehow bulky and malnourished, strung up in his posture like a wartime puppet.

He extends his long arm and pulls the door open for me. I walk in and he walks in after me. Behind us the door wheezes closed and the chimes ring.

INSIDE

The place is so bright with its fluorescent light that I have to squint. Red square tables with brown chairs and puckered red booths, all empty. Just at the counter, a thin-haired woman in a powder-pink cardigan is dipping fries into her strawberry milk-shake, and sucking on them. The clock shows past 2am.

The waitress comes toward us. She's got hazelnut-colored skin. Her mouth, though. Her mouth. A perfect cupid's bow. Carefully framed by her dark hair in a relaxed bob.

"Right this way," she says in her creamy inflection.

Nicky and I are seated at a booth against the wall and given our menus.

"Can I start you off with anything to drink?" our waitress asks.

Nicky looks up at her and pauses. She smiles at him, stretching out her cupid's bow.

NICKY ORDERS

His English is goofy. Eager. Hopeless.

"In start we have two coffee with please bring sugar and milk okay," Nicky says. The waitress writes it down dutifully in her pad.

"Also please give to us the chocolate chip pancake and also please grills cheese okay."

She adds that to her list.

HIS FACE

In the light, it's more spirit than flesh. From the sides of his cap, his dark brown hair is muzzled. His skin is gray, uneven stubble on a rickety jaw-line. It's just the eyes that make sense. Thin and blue and bootlegged in their sparkle.

LISETTE

When she's gone, Nicky tilts his head in the direction of the waitress and says, "That's Lisette. You can trust her."

"I can't even trust you," I say. "Where's Misha?"

"Misha?"

"Moshe. My brother."

Nicky reaches in his pocket and pulls out a gold chain with a dangling pendant and puts it on the table between us. Shards of light. I run my thumb over each of the six corners of the star.

"Just fucking say it, Nicky, if you're trying to tell me my brother is dead."

"*Bozhé*, Olga, you shouldn't say things like that! He's not dead. He took this off. He knew they'd just steal it where he was going."

WHERE IS HE GOING?

Lisette sets down two pearl-white mugs with deep black coffee.

"Milk and sugar are just there." She's pointing to the condiments box.

"Yes, good, we have all please goodbye," Nicky says to her hurriedly.

I look up at her. A smile begins to slide upon that beautiful mouth.

Nicky is tapping on the wooden table and leaning toward me.

"You care about your brother or not?" he says.

It might be the night. I squint and squint and squint at Nicky.

"I'm listening, aren't I?" I say.

BROTHERS

"If you're ever in any trouble, you come here and you ask for Lisette. She'll always be here when you need her."

"Okay…" I say, pouring a creamer into my coffee until it's the color of Angelina's skin.

"They've got her brother too, if it's any help to hear. His name is Rémy. He's the one who passed on Moshe's necklace."

The woman in the powder-pink cardigan creaks out of her chair and heads toward the bathroom.

Our chocolate chip pancakes and grilled cheese have arrived. Lisette is pacing away, her heels punctual on the wooden floor. Nicky is opening up the butter packet and putting the whole square onto the whipped cream on top of the pancakes, then tipping over the maple syrup till it puddles at the edges of the plate.

"I'm starving," he mumbles. "Eat, eat."

IT'S LIKE PRISON

Nicky explains as he's chewing, "...but inside out. I know. I've been to prisons. This is worse."

Nicky cuts the grilled cheese in half and offers me a piece.

I'm watching the cheese cry down the sides.

"Eat, I said," Nicky insists. "Don't draw attention."

I glance at the empty tables and Lisette refilling the napkin dispenser at the counter. I pick up the buttery charred bread and bite into the thing. Hot American cheese runs over my lip.

"Good," Nicky says, "keep eating..."

I'm wiping my mouth with a napkin. I'm taking a sip of my creamy coffee. I'm putting my fork into the chocolate chip pancakes.

"Keep eating..."

ONCE, TWICE, THRICE

"But Misha—Moshe wouldn't hurt a fly," I whisper back across the table, melted chocolate chips mixing with the cheese.

"Well he stabbed some girl once, twice, and thrice," Nicky says.

"What girl, that's not true, it can't be true!"

"Shhh..." Nicky leans in.

He's scooping the whipped cream off my side of the chocolate chip pancakes onto his.

"I telling you what I know," he whispers. "She was eighteen, from Whitefish Bay, a fancy house off Lake Drive, one of those Russians who came with money, her father's a dentist, good-looking and doesn't smell like all our fathers, you know, her mother even does school board stuff, American stuff, baking and craft paper…"

THE OTHER CHEEK

"Olga, if you turn the other cheek right now, Moshe will get hurt, and I mean *hurt*, in a way you can't even imagine."

HURT

What does it mean to *get hurt* where he is?

What does it even mean to *get hurt* where I am?

SPEAKING OF THE PILLOWCASE FULL OF SILVERWARE

Once there was this suburban hooligan picking on Misha. The things that happen in the parking lot of a mall. In the Soviet Union, there was at least some discretion and tact. If someone had it out for you, you'd be pulled into an alley, or at least into the shade, by a shrub, behind a car, for some privacy for God's sake. No one likes to be bashed up publicly, that's humiliating. But these American knuckleheads, they all want to be gangsters with their awkward guns.

So this white kid named Brendan's got a gun and he's bragging about it. He's dropping his g's and slurring and mumbling. He's acting gangster and in the suburbs it passes. He sets his eyes on Misha, tells him "you're my bitch now, bitch." Misha's in middle school. Misha doesn't say anything back. Brendan's king.

For weeks, Brendan and his crew follow Misha after school with their cars. Misha's on his bike. The guys start nicking his wheels with their bumpers. Misha's coming home scraped and bruised and the works. Finally, he spills the whole story. I tell him, Don't worry, we won't say anything to Mom and Dad. I'll fix this.

FIXING IT

It's etiquette. You never show up empty-handed when invited. Misha was invited to fight. I came with him. I took my pillowcase off my pillow and dumped our silverware into it. I figure with a good swing it could do something.

BITCHES

Misha is standing behind me saying, "Olga, please, forget it."

"Who's your babysitter, you little faggot?" Brendan asks.

He has one hand in the waistband of his pants, his baggy 2Pac T-shirt bunched around his knuckles.

"I'm his sister," I say.

"And what you got, big sis?" He points to my pillowcase.

"It's a pillowcase full of silverware," I tell him.

He pulls up his T-shirt and reveals the black gun tucked into his jeans, inside the waistband of his boxers. Even from where I'm standing, it looks fake. All guns look fake. But I know it's real. He lets his T-shirt fall back down over it.

"You know I don't hurt girls," he says. "But luckily you just a bitch, like your brother."

WAIT

Next thing I know, I'm on the ground and there's blood on Misha's white Nikes.

MISHA'S EYE

It's all red and full of blood. We have to go to the hospital. The emergency care doctor says it's permanent. My parents arrive. They tell us to wait. My father paces in the hallway and my mother eyes me with a tightened cheek. It's not rage. I can't place it. She won't speak. There is so much childhood in her parted lips.

My father comes and finds us. He is so angry, he's become gentle. I'm so ashamed, I've become arrogant. I explain diligently to both of my parents that it was not my fault. They listen. It's the only bit of love we can give each other. No one calls the police. Did I mention Brendan's dad's a cop?

When we get to see Misha, the doctor tells all of us that his left eye will never regain full sight. Misha cries. Only one eye sheds tears.

LITTLE BROTHER

He grows up to be handsome, despite everything. One blue Georgian eye. A crown of dark Jewish curls. Still pale all over. Still somewhere else.

BIG SISTER

To be alive and not to be able to.

HOW THEY START

"It's not like a physical pain," Nicky's explaining to me. "But physical pain is how you get there."

He lifts up both of his hands and opens the palms wide, facing me.

On each palm is a bulbous diagonal scar.

"This is how they start," Nicky says.

CASH

Nicky's taking cash out of his wallet.

"You got work to do," Nicky says and tilts his head toward the counter. "Lisette will set you up."

"Set me up with what?"

"Olga, your brother is counting on you."

SLEEP

When I get back home, I peel off my shoes quietly, undo my clothes, and tip-toe into the dark bedroom. There she is, my love, sleeping like an angel. I climb into bed and reach my arm around her waist under the covers. From her sweet dreams, she takes my hand and pulls it up to her chest and squeezes it against her sternum.

A JOB

I wake up early. Angelina is in the shower. When she comes out, I've already made coffee and got the box of cereal and milk out on our small kitchen table.

"Good morning," she says, drying her hair.

"I got a job," I say.

"A job?" she looks up at me with her merciful dark eyes.

Her hair is dripping and she's smiling. It's only dawn outside.

"It's at the diner on 79th and Capitol. Waitressing."

I wait a moment.

"It's just for now," I continue. "Cause I want to go back and get a real degree, you know, I really do…"

She takes a step toward me. She puts her warm hand on the side of my head.

"I'll drop you off on my way to work," she says, kissing me on my brow.

MORNING SHIFT

It's not even 7am when I'm back at the diner. I kiss Angelina goodbye and tell her not to worry, I'll take the bus home after my shift. I head toward the doors. Everything is bare now in the morning light. It smells like black coffee and fried potatoes.

Lisette comes up to me and puts a hand on my shoulder. She looks extremely well rested.

"Good to see you again," she says warmly.

I follow her behind the kitchen to the employee backroom with half-lockers. She gives me a lock and key and points to the one next to hers. This is your locker. She gets me a uniform and I put it on. I pin the nametag on my black polo shirt. "OLGA"

"Now, to start," Lisette says, "you can smile."

I stretch out my mouth and let my teeth catch some air.

GOOD TEETH

I spend the morning bringing heavy white plates of greasy food over. And black trays of sodas and coffee cups. Like Lisette says, I smile when I take their order. I smile when I bring the food. I smile when I take their money.

At lunch, I get to sit at the counter and order whatever I want from the lunch menu. I go for the club sandwich. An extra pickle. A coffee with one cream. As I'm slurping on my ice water, I hear the door chimes rattle. The woman walks over and takes a seat beside me. Her powder-pink cardigan is buttoned neatly to the top. Thin hair, brushed carefully back, gray and brown strands. She puts her dark brown purse with beige wave-like stitching on the counter. She looks over at me. Her eyes, two vows. And then she looks away.

"Hi, Sally," Lisette says to her. "Fries and a strawberry milk-shake for you this morning?"

"Oh, yes, please," the woman replies.

For a moment we are both looking in front of us, but our inner eyes are touching.

Then she turns back to me. I sip my cup with water and ice and she watches me.

"Not too cold for your teeth?" she asks.

I shake my head no.

"That means you have good teeth."

SALLY

I got five more minutes of my break when she speaks to me again.

"My name, as you may have overheard, is Sally," she says.

I'm nodding my head and finishing off my coffee.

"My name's Olga," I respond, out of politeness.

"I know," she says, "you're Moshe's sister…"

NUMBER SIX

Lisette signals to me that my break is over. I'd better clean up my plate and get back on the floor.

"Well, honey, it looks like you have to get back to work," Sally says in a sweet tone. "And when you go to the backroom, you're going to put this into locker number six."

She slides a large tan envelope folded upon itself three times and wrapped in cellophane, from her purse, to her lap, into my lap. It's oddly heavy.

"What is it?" I ask.

She takes her other hand and puts it on my own.

"It's a way for you to see your brother," she replies and gently squeezes my hand.

I take the envelope. I carry it under my shirt. I walk to the backroom. The door slides shut behind me. Inside, there is a drip in the overhead pipe.

THREE

When I come back out, she's gone.

Lisette is pointing to table three.

THE TRICK

Lisette asks me if I'm all right. I don't think I should tell her what Sally told me to do. Lisette says I look tired. Her hand is so soft all of the sudden, when she lays it on top of mine. I look away so I don't fall into the cupid's bow of her lips.

"You must be tired," she says again. "But there's a little trick that can help you.

"Whenever you're feeling this tired, you just take your thumb and your forefinger and press them together, once, twice, three times, *un, deux, trois*, once, twice, three times, *un, deux...*"

TROIS

My eyes feel wider than the sky. There is the clinking of dishes, the dry crumple of napkins, a sizzle of butter, the squirt of ketchup, the follicle buzz of the fluorescent lights. Footsteps on the wood, then on tile. The door swings shut behind me.

A row of sinks with mirrors. Three stalls. White tiles on the floor. Metal frames around each mirror. A hand dryer. A tampon dispenser. One tall black trash bin.

I go into the second stall. I undo my pants and pull down my underwear. The toilet seat is nice and cool on my butt cheeks. I'm peeing and it's feeling like a great yawn. The more I pee, the more alert I feel. The graffiti scribbled into the door peers at me. I follow it with extreme focus.

U SMELL HOE

For a good time call

TRUTH OR DARE

NUMBER 6

1991 bitches

                    NUMBER 5
                    Olga
            Ride or die
                    FUCK OFF
                    Olga
        T & S 4ever
        NUMBER 4
                        Go to hell
                    Olga
    NUMBER 3
                        Olga
        2 hot 2 be single
                    NUMBER 2
                        Olga,
                        Olga,
                        Help me

DON'T

"Olga, please help me..." The voice is coming from outside the stall.

I know it. I know him. It's Misha, Misha! I'm pulling up my pants and reaching for the hook of the stall, "I'm coming, Misha—"

"Don't!" Misha's voice says. "Don't come out."

"What?"

"Please... don't open the door, I... I don't want you to see me... like this."

"Like what?" I'm leaning my head against the stall door, "Misha... are you okay?" There are footsteps on the other side, two of them on the tiles.

"It's Moshe. My name is Moshe..."

"*Moshe*, yes, Moshe."

"Did you get my necklace?"

"Yeah, I got it…"

"Olga…"

"Yeah?"

"I didn't mean to…"

"To what?"

"…once… twice… thrice…"

"The girl off Lake Drive? I'm coming out—"

"No!" The footsteps scurry back.

My hand is frozen at the latch.

"Please… just… do what I say… please."

"Okay… okay, Misha—"

"It's Moshe!" he yelps.

My finger is touching the metal of the latch.

"*Moshe…*" I whisper.

A drip.

A drip, drip.

Not from the overhead pipe.

A drip, drip.

It's from my brother. From my little brother.

I crouch, one palm on the cool stall door, the other on the tiles. I'm peeking beneath the stall. I see two shoes. White Nikes. Misha's white Nike's. And down. A drip, one long drip is dropping. A drop of blood. Falling. Like a tiny red bird that's lost its wings. It splatters on the toe of his sneaker.

I jump up at the door. I flip the latch and push the stall wide open.

"Mishenka!"

There, before me. White ceramic sinks with mirrors, each showing half of me.

SEE

"That's the trick." Lisette removes her hand from mine, then raises it to my face.

"Don't you feel more awake already?"

WHEN MY SHIFT IS OVER THE SKY IS YELLOW WITH EXHAUSTED SUN

I wait at the bus stop.

THE BUS DROPS ME OFF AT THE CORNER

I walk to the stop sign. I turn at the shrubs.

At our building, I pull out my keys and beep myself in.

AT HOME

I take a shower. Hot and steamy until I'm clean.

ANGELINA COMES HOME

She changes into a green dress and takes her hair down.

The sight of her makes me want to fall onto my knees. I imagine it as a scene. Ouch. I hear my knees crack. I squint and the scene is gone.

I go out onto the balcony and have a smoke.

DINNER

Tonight, we're in Brown Deer having dinner with Angelina's parents, Carmita and Bud.

"Well, how was your first day of work?" Mama Carmita is asking me. "Angie told me you got a new job…"

"The diner on 79th and Capitol," I say, "yeah," then scoop some peas onto my plate.

YES, YES, YES

Mama Carmita is a nurse like Angelina, except for the elderly, at Sunrise Care Center at South 43rd. She's giving me a smile. I can't look her in the eyes. I love her more than my own mom. I know I shouldn't weigh love against itself. But I weigh love against itself. Little questions come and find me. Questions, like: do I love Angelina more than Misha? I'm afraid the answer is yes.

Yes, yes, yes.

BUD AND CARMITA

Bud's cutting a slice of the pork roast for me. He's Angelina's rose-skinned father. Originally from Lafayette in Indiana. He's got a mustache like Stalin. In America, it shows the type of man who's sensitive to cheddar. He's a software engineer at M & I Data Services on Water Street. Bud speaks in short sentences. He holds Carmita by the waist.

"Thanks, Bud," I say, taking the slice.

There's also sofrito rice, steaming its blend of peppers, onion, garlic, and cilantro, and there's tostones that were left-over from last night and a bowl of cooked sweet peas, because Mama Carmita knows I love peas.

CNN is on mute in the living room. More of a lamp. A source of light in the household. Cause Carlos, that's Angelina's brother, he's in the army. Carlos has been deployed twice to Afghanistan, Jalalabad, and now to the Nangahar province. We all sit together and watch CNN. Mama Carmita gives firm hugs. Bud cooks heavy meals.

THE ARMY

There's not much you can do against the decree of a childhood mission. That was Carlos. Carmita and Bud can't say where he got it in his head. He's been waiting to join the army since he was in elementary school.

There are boys who are born to be brothers. They are drawn to an extreme kinship by intuition. Their asylum, communal loss. (I keep this thought to myself.)

When Angelina or Bud or Carmita talk about Carlos, I get the sense that he's all alone in time and they are trying to synchronize him with their words.

KINDRED

I don't know if I'm projecting. I think Carlos and Nicky could have looked after each other…

WORRY

Carmita and Bud worry about Carlos. When I'm with them, I want to worry about Carlos. But the only worry that stirs in me is for the person who's here, by my side. Angelina.

I WONDER

Does Mama Carmita love Angelina more than Carlos?

(Yes, yes, yes…)

DINNER TALK

Angelina is sitting across from me. She catches me looking at her. She gives me a private smile. I catch it and lock it up greedily. Bud's mustache is shifting as he chews. Carmita takes a sip of her Tropicana juice. I am back to studying Angelina's face.

Carmita starts up the conversation. She says Carlos is due soon for time off. Bud confirms that Carlos is due soon for time off. Angelina wonders when exactly Carlos will come home. Bud and Carmita and Angelina take guesses that aren't precise at all. Soon, we all agree. It's soon.

PEAS

"Olgalita, honey, do you want more peas?" Carmita asks. She is holding the metal spoon above the tan ceramic bowl. Bright green peas like syllables. Carmita scoops the peas onto my plate. They go tumbling, rolling. I collect them in a pile near a slice of pork in a puddle of oil and herbs.

I forget things when I'm eating peas. To listen. To answer. To participate in dinner talk.

All of the sudden, Angelina is laughing in unison with Mama Carmita. Their laughter is so beautiful. I feel as if I'm being lifted and taken up to heaven.

WE DRIVE HOME

After dinner in Angelina's dark blue sedan. My hands are trembling. I fold them into my thighs so that Angelina doesn't see. It's drizzling on the black road.

The windshield wipers erase us from the outside.

Angelina places her hand on my knee.

"You were very quiet at dinner," she says.

I am thinking to myself, I will do anything for love.

NIGHT

Shoes off. My stringy hair.

Angelina's in the shower.

TEXT MESSAGE

From Nicky.

<GOOD JOB TODAY>

What.

What have I done?

MY ANGEL

The bathroom door clicks open. Angelina steps out. Her hair is wet. It's dripping down her bare collarbone. Her torso, wrapped in a gray towel.

What.

What have I done?

WHAT I WANT

I leave my phone on the bed and walk over to her. I squeeze her into me.

We are face to face. My lips. Her lips. And space for. What I want.

I WANT

To break through the skin of this lifetime.

OFF, OFF

I pull her damp towel off. I'm smearing whatever is left of my lipstick on her clean cheek. What I want. I want.

She's got me on the bed. Ice and earth. Her forehead. Her tongue. Her breasts. Her perfect heat. What I want.

A SIMPLE SONG

The next morning a bird sings. It's a simple song. My hand still lays between Angelina's thighs.

WORK

Angelina drops me off at the diner again. The door chimes when I enter. Lisette is at the cash register. She smiles like clockwork. My eyes feel so dry.

When I walk over, she lifts up a plastic cup with a teal lid.

"We're having a mandatory staff drug test today," Lisette says and hands me the cup.

HALF FULL

In the bathroom, I crouch over the bowl with the cup between my legs. I follow the graffiti scribbled on the door. It's quiet. I get up and peek under the stall just in case. No white Nikes. I pee into the cup.

I come out of the bathroom with my duty completed. A male police officer comes toward me. A balding redhead. Freckles. Goatee.

"Are you Olga Bokuchava...?"

"Yes," I say. "You need my urine, officer?"

HALF EMPTY

When I reach the cup of urine toward him, he lunges at me. He grabs the cup from my hand and pulls my arm behind my back. Then the other.

"What are you—" I try to call out.

A female police officer with her hair slicked back in a bun steps toward me. She's holding an envelope wrapped in cellophane.

"Is this yours, ma'am?"

I try to keep my wits about me. Both my arms are twisted at my back.

"Officer, I've never seen that before in my life." I decide to play it cool.

"Then what was it doing in your locker," the officer asks.

"My locker?"

"Number six. That's your locker, ma'am."

OH NO

The officer unwraps cellophane off the envelope, unfolds it and pulls out a brownish-smudged handkerchief. She unwraps the sticky handkerchief. There, in her hand, like a fresh-cut flower, is a thick kitchen knife.

"Ms. Bokuchava… you understand that *this* is a murder weapon."

UN, DEUX, TROIS

They drag me through the dining area. The customers turn their heads and look at me.

"Lisette," I shout out.

She's behind the counter. She looks at me too. Her cupid's bow is pinched.

"You have to tell them," I yelp. "There was this woman… her name is Sally!"

Lisette doesn't say anything. They are pulling me and she's watching.

"Lisette!" I yell, "Lisette!!"

Lisette mouths with satiny precision, *un, deux, trois…*

ONE CALL

At the station, they cuff me to the chair. I'm allowed one call. They put the telephone at the edge of the desk. They hand me the receiver. I should call Angelina. My fingers drift from one number to the next. Numbers from the middle of the night. I'm braiding them together.

BAD LUCK

"*Da?*" he husks on the phone.

"Nicky, I've been arrested," I spit out.

"Yes, Olga," he replies. "Go with it."

"…go with it?"

"Just do as they say."

"Nicky, they're saying I murdered someone!"

"She'll contact you soon, don't worry."

"Who? Who?"

"Oh," he pauses. "Sally."

Then his line is dead. And it's bad luck to talk into a dead receiver.

NOT HERE

The guard pushes me down a cement hallway.

"Don't I get a lawyer?" I squeal.

"Not here," she replies, prodding me forth.

THE ROOM

It has a metal door. A code box. The guard types in the code. A small light flashes green and the door springs open. She nudges me and I walk in. The door closes behind us. Inside, another small light turns red.

A metal table. A white plastic basket. A camera in the corner pointed at us.

"Take off your clothes and put them in the basket," the officer says.

I peel myself like a potato. I feel shyer by the layer. I'm firm and raw. One hand over my groin. The other covering my chest.

"Your jewelry," she says.

I lift my hands to my earlobes and take out each gold stud. I put them carefully into the basket on top of my clothes.

"Your necklace." She's losing patience with me.

"What necklace?" I mumble.

"Don't provoke me, Bokuchava, the one you're wearing."

I look down at my collarbone. The dangling star. *Misha Moshe Misha Moshe.* I put it in the basket.

"When will I get it back?" I ask.

"When they say you can leave," she answers.

"How long will that take?"

"That depends."

"On what?"

She thinks for a moment. Then, there is a bloom in her face.

"On… Mercy. Faith. Justice. Blood Type. Star sign. Caste system. Poetry," she says.

SMALL

I'm wearing state-issued underwear and bra. Wall-white. They smell sour and over-washed. Over them, light blue cotton pants. White T-shirt. Light blue zip-up hoodie.

They got my sizes all wrong.

The underwear is loose at the crotch.

The bra straps are uneven.

The waistband of the pants is stretched out.

The hoodie is missing its draw-string.

My body is a state-issued shape.

DEAD END

She takes me down one last hallway. Concrete walls. Dead end. There, a room. Not a room. A cell. A metal toilet, no cover. A sink. Bunk beds. On the bottom one, there's someone. A body. A woman. Her knees are up against her chest, hands folded across her face to block the light.

"Get up, Tarasova," the officer says her way, "and say *hi* to your new roommate."

I'm pushed inside and the gate is locked.

TANYA TARASOVA

She doesn't get up until the officer has left. When she does, she lowers her feet to the floor then rises. It's somehow theological. White socks, yellowing at the toes. Her blue sweat pants are fitted.

Her sweatshirt shows off her tits. She's got blue eye-shadow on, and blue irises inside her dark, sunken eyes. Her hair's behind her ears, long and brown and shiny, as if it's squinting.

I see two gold earrings in the shape of hearts.

TWO HEARTS

"They let you keep your earrings?" I ask Tanya.

She smoothes out her hair without looking at me.

A PROMISE

Finally, she lifts her eyes. Then she lifts her hand. Then she extends her square-tipped teal acrylic fingernail at my face.

"I'm going to fucking kill you," she whispers.

STAY

She tells me. I crouch down against the wall. Near the toilet. Just in case. It smells like steel. And pee.

I stay there for a long time. I stay there even when Tanya lies back down on her bunk. She sleeps. I stay.

MUSIC

That makes no sound accompanies me.

I prop my head up with my elbow on the steel toilet seat. The bars make shadows. The moon runs across them and brings them to life. Several times I think it's Angelina. Tip-toeing. But it's just moon playing the prison like a harp.

SLEEP

Tanya's snoring now. I've got my arms around my knees. I think about Angelina. What she thinks about me, absent. What she thinks about. And me. Absent.

MISTAKE

It's morning and the guard brings us two trays. Cottony toast. A juice box of orange juice concentrate. A sausage patty. And a mush of eggs.

Tanya takes her tray on her lap. She eats the food with small pinches of her fingers. I say I'm not hungry, out loud—to whomever is listening. I yell out that I want to make a call and I won't eat until I get it. The guard tells me that I already made my call. I yell out that I want to make another call. The guard says that's not possible. I only get one. Tanya says that I need to shut the fuck up already and eat my fucking food.

I start yelling, "Angelina! Angelina!" Tanya rolls her eyes and covers her ears. Her long teal nails crown her temples. I grab the bars and lunge toward the guard.

"Angelina! Angelina!" I yell at the guard's face.

The guard pulls out her baton. She strikes it once on the bar near my hand. My fingers flinch.

"Your knuckles are next," the guard says.

I look at her. She looks at me. We see other things.

"Annnnnngeeeelllinnnnnaaaaaa!!" I yell out.

The guard flips the side of her baton at my hand grasping the bar.

White, sudden white, surges through my head. I stagger.

I'm squeezing my eyes and squeezing my hand.

"Ouch—" I manage to gasp, as if humiliated by breath.

HAPPINESS

"Happy now?" Tanya says.

My hand is pulsing with frost.

ZABASTOVKA

Tanya has craters where she has pecked her food. Mine is untouched.

"Your fucking *zabastovka* won't get you anything," Tanya mumbles.

"I'm not protesting." I look up.

"Whatever," Tanya says dryly.

She moves her tongue in her mouth and sends a wad of spit onto my tray.

MY PLACE
It's by the steel toilet. I sit there. I stand there. I sleep there.

I YELL BETWEEN THE BARS
When I hear footsteps. There are often footsteps. There is rarely someone.

WHAT'S YOUR SHIT STORY?
Suddenly Tanya's got questions for me. I don't answer. She hits the bunk with a flat hand.

"Bitch, I'm trying to get to know you."

I swallow and lift my gaze.

"I don't want you to get to know me."

IT'S MY FIRST NIGHT HORIZONTAL
I climb up to my bunk and I sleep there.

Tanya's picking at her nails. She doesn't notice or she doesn't care.

IN MY SLEEP
There's a child in the corner. In the dark. In our cell. There's a child reciting with the voice of a bird. There are no birds outside. There is no morning light, just light without time, making

shadows through the bars. I tilt my head. They make telephone wires. If only I could get one more phone call. If only, Angelina.

There's a child reciting under his breath. His breath is made of the horizon. There's a child reciting a poem in Russian. There is water everywhere. It is the Russian language. I close my eyes and open my eyes. He is still there.

There is a child in the corner, in the dark, in the storm.

THE STORM

"A lonely sail is flashing white
  Amidst the blue mist of the sea..."
  the boy is reciting.

THE LONE BOAT

Is restless.

IT COULD

Stay in the gleaming sunlight. Stay in the calm azure waters.

AND YET

"...it seeks out a storm
  As if in storms it could find peace."

WAKE UP

I'm rolling my head right and left. I'm trying to get myself out of the dream. The heavy-handed dream that is pulling me under his voice. I'm twisting behind my eyelids. Wake up, Olga.

GEMS

My eyes burst open. There, near our steel toilet, shivering in his little green swimsuit, the boy has droplets of water all over his body. They shine like gems.

THE LITTLE BOY WHIMPERS
"Pozhalusta, tyotya..." Please, missus.

HIS NOSE IS RUNNY
Slow, hanging drips. The mucus stays on his upper lip. It shimmers like crushed diamonds.

"...I'm drowning..." he mewls.

OH NO
I'm pressed against the wall, all quiet, all eyes.

The bunk shifts.

SHE'S UP TOO
"That's Dima," Tanya chaffs, "the old lady's son."

"...from floor six?" I'm shivering now.

"Yes, yes, yes, you dumb ass, *blyad*!" Tanya says.

DIMA TAKES A STEP TOWARD OUR BUNKS
"Dimochka," Tanya makes her voice high and strange.

"You wanna play?" she chirps. "Let's play, *malish*."

Tanya punches my top bunk. "Hey, Olga, play with Dima!"

I AM SHAKING MY HEAD INTO SMALLNESS
No, no, no thanks.

THE TOUCH GAME
"Dimochka's just looking for a little touch. Isn't that right, *malish*? Except that Dimochka's touch—" Tanya lets out a thick laugh.

I WANNA PLAY WITH MISSUS OLGA
Dima pipes up. His words crystallize out of his mouth and make the air sting.

OUCH
I squint because my eyes are tingling.

COME PLAY
Tanya shouts.

WAIT
I'm clutching my wrists into my neck and turning my head into the wall.

FUCKING PLAY WITH DIMOCHKA
Tanya's banging on my bunk.

My hands are tucked tightly between my thighs. The right still sore from the guard's baton. The pain pulses into the left. I squeeze them closer. They share the pain.

DIMA STARTS RUNNING TOWARD ME
His whole body lifts up as his legs cycle in the air.

MY HANDS
My hands are the limbs I'm losing in evolution—

MY HANDS

Slip out from between my thighs like a ribbon being unknotted.

HE'S HOVERING AT MY BUNK

His wet hair, touching the cement ceiling. He opens his mouth and smiles with all his teeth. His smile prickles my eyes. I shut them.

MY HANDS ARE CLASPED IN FRONT OF ME

It burns.

FIRE AND ICE

The heat between them.

THE HEAT BETWEEN THEM

It's a solid thing.

I'M CLASPING A SOLID THING

"Open your eyes, missus," the boy says.
    My cheeks go numb and the tip of my nose stings.

EYES WIDE OPEN

Hands closed shut.
    I look down at them.
    He's looking there too.
    We are both looking at my hands.

THE KITCHEN KNIFE
I'm holding.
   The boy shows all his teeth at once.

THE BOY
A thousand diamonds.

MAKE HIM STOP
Razors. Shoreline. Sunlight.

THE LAST WAVE
Seagulls cut stones with their voices.

MY HANDS RAISED ABOVE MY HEAD
"Once, twice, thrice, missus!" the boy is screaming.

THE KNIFE RAISED ABOVE MY HEAD
Make him stop!

THE PENDULUM
Oh no. Oh no.

THE KNIFE SWINGS DOWN
It pierces deep into something that feels like everything.

LOOK NOW
My eyes push out droplets of the poem.

AS IF IN STORMS
It could find peace.

OLGA

Tanya shifts in her bunk below me.

"Quit your fucking screaming," she tells me, "and go to sleep."

GOOD NIGHT

Pain without meaning.

IT'S BREAKFAST TIME

The guard brings us two trays. I don't touch mine. I can't open or close my hands. I study my palms. There. A strike across each one, swelling like a burn.

Tanya picks at her food diligently. I sit with my two stiff hands on my lap.

MY DAYS

I stay still. They go by.

BIRDS

Tanya swears at me. Tanya threatens me. Tanya tells me that I'm worthless.

HOPE

For a second, I feel it.

There are footsteps beyond our cell.

They have a weight to them.

VISITOR

"Tarasova!" The guard is banging her baton on the bars.

Tanya smiles in a full rectangle. The guard smiles back. On each side of the bars, their smiles are an equation.

I study it. I can't quite solve it.

MATH
You don't exist. You don't exist.

HEY, BABY
The guard puts her baton back against her thigh in one low swing. There is a guy behind her. Tommy Hilfiger hoodie. Jeans bunch around his chicken legs. He lifts his face to the light.

"Brendan!" Tanya jumps up.

"Hey, baby."

SHIT
I am turning my face away, hoping he won't notice me.

FACES
They are tonguing each other through the bars. His hands grope her ass cheeks. The guard taps on the bar with her baton. "I don't want to tell you again," she says.

"Damn, okay," Brendan says, "all right…"

He reaches into his pocket and hands the guard a roll of bills. She looks at it, slides it into her pocket and nods.

He leans his face through the bars again and whispers, "You got what I want, baby?"

"Sure do…" she exhales.

They go back to tonguing and I can see Brendan has an erection. He's squeezing Tanya's breasts and she's cupping his package.

BITCH

"Time's up, lovebirds," the guard says, twisting the roll of bills in her pocket. She bangs on the bars again for them to separate.

When Brendan takes his face off Tanya, it lands on me.

"Who the fuck is that," Brendan stamps.

"Who?" Tanya says. "Oh that, that's my new cellie."

"I know her, she's that bitch's sister."

"What bitch?"

"You know. That bitch-ass bitch. Misha."

"It's Moshe," I pipe up.

Tanya turns back to me.

"So that's Moshe's sister…"

I pinch my eyes at her.

She turns back to Brendan.

"Ignore her, baby," she says, "don't waste our time on her."

"Yeah, okay, just be careful. Heard she real thirsty for cunt."

"Are you jealous, Brennie…" Tanya puckers her mouth.

"I'm fucking serious, she's fucking going to go down on you in your sleep, baby, I swear."

Tanya looks back at me and smiles, then turns to Brendan.

"And what are you gonna do about it?" she says in a baby voice.

Brendan flinches his arm up and bangs the bar with his fist. "Fuuuuuuuuuuuuuuuuuuuuuck!" he screams.

The guard taps her baton into her palm. "Quiet down."

Brendan turns to the guard. "You gotta switch her out, my baby's locked up with a psycho dyke!"

"Quiet down, I said," the guard repeats.

Brendan turns red, squeezing his fists against his temples.

"Breathe, baby, breathe," Tanya is saying.

Brendan unclasps his hands and lets out a sloppy exhale. He begins to whimper.

"Shhh…" she says. "I'm just kidding, Brennie baby, you know

I love dick, especially yours, and as soon as I'm out, I'll suck you off so good, won't I?"

Brendan picks up his solemn head.

"Okay, but," he says in a grave tone, "you stay strong for us both, baby."

"I will, Brennie, I will," Tanya says.

They tongue each other again until the guard hits the bars with her baton and Brendan has to leave.

SO WHAT

"You didn't fucking tell me you were Moshe's sister," Tanya says, still looking through the bars where Brendan once stood.

Somehow the sun has already set and we haven't even had lunch, or dinner.

My stomach is growling and she is turning around.

WAVES

I don't know if it's the waves of hunger. Or the waves of nausea. Or the waves, in her eyes. Tanya.

She's looking at me—her eyes waver like water. Distant upheaval. Her irises reciting that poem. Lermontov's *Parus odinokiy.*

THE LONE SAILBOAT

That poem about the lone sailboat that leaves the safe waters and goes willingly into the heart of a storm.

BECAUSE

What is life, if you cannot willingly go into the heart of the storm. What is life, if you cannot willingly storm someone's heart. What is life, if you cannot willingly leave safe waters.

ACCUSATIONS

"Your brother," Tanya's eyes heat up, "is a bad fucking person."

"That's not true."

"Well he stabbed me," she says and takes a step toward me, "Once… twice… thrice…"

She points to her own body with one curved finger. Stomach. Ribs. Heart.

YOU'RE A LIAR

"Do I have to spell it out? Your brother is a murderer. What a psycho fucking family."

IT MUST HAVE BEEN AN ACCIDENT

"He didn't mean it."

MALCHIK

"He sure as fucking hell meant it. I was there. I was there with my bestie, Svetlana. It was him, your brother, and his weirdo mother-fucking friend."

SHE WAS SO SCARED

Svetlana.

SHE WAS SCARED TO DIE

My bestie.

SHE WAS SCREAMING SCREAMING SCREAMING

"You wouldn't fucking get it."

YOUR BROTHER
"He ruined my life."

I CAN'T FIT IT ALL TOGETHER
Tanya grabs my jaw with her fingers. Her long nails dent into my cheeks.

"I'm on to you," she grits.

YEAH
She takes her hand off my face. I stretch out my jaw and rub my chin.

"You expect me to believe you're dead?" I say real low.

"Don't give a fuck what you believe," Tanya says. "I won't be nobody's stank-ass joke."

A MESSAGE
I lift my chin. I look at her straight in the eyes.

"*Idi... na... khuyi,*" I tell her nice and slow in Russian. *Go fuck yourself.*

SHE GRABS ME BY THE THROAT
Her thumb is in my voice box.

NOW, NOW
"Now, now, now," Tanya says.

NOW?
I'm struggling to breathe.

WELL NOW

"So, you think just cause your brother's a psycho, that makes you a tough cunt, huh?"

NO

I'm grabbing at my neck.

NO, NO

I don't know why she's so strong.

YES

"You want me to show you a little something about the natural world order?"

FUCK YES

She's squeezing into my larynx.

FUCK ME

"You're a worthless little shit. I do what I want with you. I'm the fucking psycho here. You got that, *suka*?"

WHAT'S THAT

My eyes are bulging out of my skull.

   "You want me to rape you with my fist?"

AMEN, YOU TOUGH CUNT

I'm choking on the lack.

SHE LETS GO

I drop to the floor.

GASPING AT HER FEET
"Bet you'd like that, wouldn't you?"

POEM
She lies back on her bunk and pulls her sweatpants down. She tells me to look where she's pointing. She's pointing between her legs. She's wearing a neon pink lace thong. Its threads are glowing on her shade-less skin. She pulls her thong to one side.
    "Well…?"
    Her two lips are pale and gleaming.

HORIZON
"See. I'm wet all the fucking time."

SHADOW
"Help me," Tanya says.

THE OPEN SKY
She takes her fingers and pulls her lips apart.

PARUS
Peeking out.
    I'm still catching my breath.

NAUTICAL
The eye.
    I'm still on all fours.

NAUGHTY
The storm.
"Come here, I said."

DEATH
She lays her head back and closes her eyes.

OLGA, OLGA, OLGA
"Suck the darkness out of me."

LOVEBIRDS
"Well, well..." the guard is swinging her baton at her hip. "What do we have here..."

Tanya pulls her pants up and looks at me. "Get the fuck up, you gross bitch."

I lift myself off my knees.

THE GUARD GIVES TANYA A WINK
"Having a good time together?"

TANYA LOOKS AT THE GUARD HEAD ON
"I'm going to pluck that eyeball out of your eye and shove it up your constipated ass if you ever wink at me again."

THE GUARD SMACKS THE BARS WITH HER BATON
The metal echoes off tune.

"Watch your language, Tarasova," the guard shouts.

MY LANGAUGE?

"This language?" Tanya says. "This piece of shit junk-ass language isn't mine."

MERCY

The guard taps her baton on the bars with a sly mouth.

"Back off Tarasova, I'm not here for you. Bokuchava!" she yells at me. "You have a visitor."

ONCE, TWICE

I jerk up from myself. Tanya's gritting her teeth.

"Move your ass, Bokuchava," the guard says, "I said you have a visitor."

I step forth warily. Tanya watches me.

MY VISITOR

Powder-pink cardigan buttoned to the top.

"Hi, Olga," she says.

SALLY

Tanya jumps up. She grips the bars with her hands.

"Sally, Sally!" she chirps off key.

KNUCKLES DOWN

The guard yells at Tanya. She takes her hands off the bars.

"Visitor's not for you, Tarasova, it's for your girlfriend," the guard says. "I said, step back."

TANYA STEPS BACK

"When I get out of here," she whispers, "I'm going to do all the things to you that stretch out your void."

BACK DOWN

The guard hits the bars with her baton.

"You don't scare me, Tarasova, you know why?"

"Why," Tanya cringes.

"Cause you are never, never, never getting outta here, my little one."

WELL

Sally clears her throat.

"That's enough of that, wouldn't we all agree?" Sally proposes.

WHATEVER YOU SAY, CRAZY MAMA

Tanya mutters.

THAT'S RIGHT

Sally continues. She looks at me.

"Tanya has a strong character. She calls me Crazy Mama, though I am still not so clear as to why. But I prefer Sally, if you don't mind."

"Yeah, yeah, yeah," Tanya interrupts. "You here to tell us a joke or what?"

COME ON

Tanya grinds her teeth.

"Tell us a fucking joke, Crazy Mama."

INCANTATION

"Joke, joke, joke!!" Tanya is chanting.

SHHH

Sally puts her finger to her lips.

"Sure, honey, one joke for you and your new roommate."

I DON'T WANT TO HEAR A JOKE

"I don't know you," I tell Sally, "and I don't like you."

"Shut the fuck up," Tanya tells me.

I WANT TO GET OUT OF HERE

"Top news…" Tanya rolls her eyes.

JUST LET ME MAKE ONE CALL

"Step away from the bars," the guard tells me. "Let your visitor tell you a joke."

FOR FUCK'S SAKE

Tanya yells. "I'm gonna fucking kill everyone here if I don't hear a fucking joke right now!"

THE JOKE

"A squirrel goes to a therapist," Sally begins, "and the squirrel says, Doc, is it true that you are what you eat? Sure, the therapist says, yes. Yes? Yes. The squirrel sighs, defeated. What's wrong? the therapist asks the squirrel. Well, Doc, the squirrel replies, in that case, I'm completely nuts."

THE GUARD IS LAUGHING

It's all splinters and phlegm.

TANYA IS LAUGHING

Her laughter is dressed-up and loud. It has the gloomy confidence of a sacred procession gone wrong. A wedding between the henchman and the decapitated.

WHAT'S YOUR PROBLEM

"You don't think it's funny or what? Or you too much of a dumbass to get it?"

LEAVE HER ALONE, TANYA

Sally says. "You got your joke."

HONEY

Sally's voice is delicate.

It's directed to me.

"I told you," I say to Sally, "I don't trust you, whoever you are."

A SECRET

Sally whispers through the bars, "You're going to have to trust whoever I am."

DOWN, DOWN

Sally tells Tanya to stay. Sally tells me to go.

I'm pulled out of my cell and the guard drags me by the arm behind Sally. Hallway into hallway. There is a dead end. Another cell. Two empty bunks. A body in shadow. In the corner. Crouching beside the steel toilet. He lifts up his head. Pale face with those dark curls and his one blank eye.

"Misha..." I whisper through the bars.

His good eye finds me.

I'M HERE TO HELP YOU

"Leave me alone," he says through his hands.

"I know, I know, I know I should have come earlier. I should have come looking for you, Mishenka…"

"Fuck, Olga. My name is Moshe now."

TIME

"Yes," I say, "yes, I'm sorry, yes, *Moshe*…"

MOSHE

"They're saying you stabbed somebody…" I tell him.

He drops his head and covers it with his palms.

"I think I've broken the sixth commandment. I've dropped it and broken it. It was my favorite one."

ARE YOU SURE

"*Moshe*, listen to me, I think you were set up," I say hurriedly. "I was set up too!"

BROTHER, SISTER

He takes his hands off his face and stands up. He extends his arms forward, spreading his fingers out wide. There is a moment I think he is reaching for me, my little brother is reaching for me. But then the light catches his hands and I see it. There, on each palm, two deep burns, puckered with heat.

"It's too late, now, sister," he says.

HIS ONE BLUE EYE

He drops his arms to his sides and digs his chin into his collarbone.

"What is it, brother, you can tell me…"

His head is squirming on his shoulders.

Sally clears her throat again.

LOOK AT ME

"Honey, your brother is a murderer."

HIS HEAD IN HIS HANDS, HIS HEAD BETWEEN HIS KNEES

"It's not your fault, I know it's not!"

"Well, honey, that's not really the truth, now is it?"

Sally tries to take my hand. I flip it away.

"Moshe, it's just that the whole world let you down. Isn't that what happened?"

MY BROTHER LIFTS HIS HEAD

"Olga," he breathes out. "Go to Hell."

NO, NO, NO

My arms like serpents through the bars.

GO TO HELL!

My brother's crying.

GO TO HELL, OLGA!

The whole hallway screams at me.

BOTH MY SHOULDERS

Gripped. Sally on one side. The guard on the other.

They are pulling me away.

HALLWAYS
Always hallways.

I'M MOVING BACKWARD INTO DARKNESS
Back, back, back.

I DON'T KNOW WHOSE BODY THEY ARE PULLING
Is it mine?
　　Could it be mine?

THEY LET GO
I fall and I'm folded over myself.
　　The floor is different.
　　"Parting is such sweet sorrow…"
　　It's Sally's voice.
　　"Is it sweet, Sally?"

THAT'S WHAT THEY SAY AND IT MAKES THE DARKNESS SMALL ENOUGH TO SWALLOW
The guard is making one long wet kissy sound.

JUST LIKE THAT
"You're free to go, Bokuchava," the guard says.
　　The door closes and the small light goes red.
　　The officer is holding a white plastic basket with my clothes folded in a pile.

YOU'RE FREE TO GO
But no one's free to go.
　　No one, no one, no one.
　　You, Bokuchava.

Free.
You gross-ass bitch.

GOODBYE, HONEY
Sally's voice but no Sally.

GET DRESSED
The officer tells me.

WILDERNESS
The holes in Tanya's eyes.
You don't fucking know me…

OLD POTATO
I'm putting my old clothes back on my body. Peels of an old story. Pants on. Sweater hanging on my body. Earrings, those. One in each lobe.

"Here," the officer juts out her hand.

In her palm, the gold necklace shimmers.

"Looks like it's Fate," she adds.

Her teeth are thick and pearly.

THE DANGLING STAR
I clasp the necklace around my neck.

The officer nods at the camera. The light flashes green and the door slides open.

NICKY NICKY NIKOLAI

FIRST OF ALL
All my life I've been taking one-twos.

IF IT WASN'T
From my late daddy, then it was from his brother, my uncle Borya who stayed with us when his wife took his two daughters and hiked it over to her parents in Moscow. Uncle Borya had a lot to say about his so-called "city-bitches"—but I was the only one in the household who was small enough to be hit.

MY LATE DADDY WAS THE COOL ONE
He could flick a blade in his mouth with his tongue before putting it back into the razor. His brother was the stinky one, always smoking or farting.

ALL I WANTED
Mathematics was my paradise. I didn't want to go outside in the courtyard with the *malchiki* loitering. I wanted to stay in and solve equations. One after another after another. Each one I solved, I disappeared. Each one I solved, I went farther away into a heavenly body.

EARTHLY LIFE
A hand would reach in and pull me out and close the door behind me. *Go play outside for fuck's sake.*
   I'd be in the courtyard with the *malchiki*.

CIRCUMSTANCES
Uncle Borya met another woman. She had a son from her first marriage. He was a little thing, a chair cushion. The poor kid took my place.

I HAD MY SHARE
My daddy passed away, rest his soul. His liver was not as cool as him.

MY MOTHER
She loved me like a sponge. The *malchiki* taunted me.
    For her love and for my father's early death.

ONE-TWOS
The *malchiki* said, Let's box.

HEY
Come on, they said, let's throw some one-twos.

FOR FUCK'S SAKE, NICKY
I said, No thanks.

THEN THERE WAS DIRT IN MY EYES
Leave me alone, I said.

I WAS REPEATING MYSELF
The *malchiki* grabbed me and they ripped my shirt. I couldn't see who was who.

IT'S NEVER GOOD TO REPEAT YOURSELF
They pushed me to-and-fro. My own arms and legs, redundant and tongue-tied.

THE COSMOS
I fell to the ground and made a ball of my body. They kicked me from all directions like a zodiac. I put my arms over my head. I counted the one-twos. One-two one-two one-two one-two... until there was just zero of me throbbing.

INFINITE FRACTAL CURVE
From the dirt and dust, I saw a dog.

A BIG DOG
Gray and white and brown. Ears up like arrows. Dark eyes, focused on me.

THE BOYS LEFT
I took my hands off my head. He came toward me. His flesh and fur swayed as he walked. I don't know where he came from. I'd never seen him around before.

HE NUDGED HIS NOSE AT MY KNEES
He began licking my slack palm laying in the dirt.

NATURAL NUMBERS
People don't always know if you're good or bad. Animals do.

I GOT UP AND STARTED WALKING
Bloody and sore and without thought.

He walked at my side. He breathed in tempo with me.

AT MY BUILDING
I stopped. I looked down at him.
  "Heya, Vaska," I finally said.
  It was henceforth his name.
  He wagged his tail.

I SAT ON THE CURB AND STROKED HIS HEAD
I was killing time. I didn't want to show my mother my face.

THE EMPTY SET
We seek ourselves in the eyes of others. For so many years, I couldn't see love, only fear and fatigue and disgust. My mother, my late father, my schoolmaster and teachers, the neighbors, the other kids, boys and girls, and men and women. I looked at them and it looked like hate and I saw myself.

TOUCH
I don't know where it happened, I didn't see it. Touch, I mean, touch. Not pain.

AXIOMS
As for the violence, I guess I couldn't care the way I was supposed to. Why was it important to know who smacks whom? Why are all the boys and men so caught up on it? So proud that *they* smacked *me*.

  So I told them, I don't care if you smack me. Anyway, we are both just the smack.

THE HIGH OF A NEW THEORUM

There was this new baby born on my floor, across the hall. She was very quiet. She didn't cry much at all. Just looked. She looked at everything as if she could put it in her mouth, suck on it to distinguish the shape of the soul.

That was you, Olga.

You glimpsed at me and I glimpsed at you. It wasn't a glimpse. You were teething on me with your dark eyes. You were tasting my soul.

Well, what did it taste like?

MIKHAIL LERMONTOV

Poet and painter. His verses just stick. Like oil colors that bring waves to the edges of the canvas.

MY FAVORITE POEM

It was that one everyone had to learn in school. The other kids mocked its verses. *A stupid sailboat chooses to go into a storm when it could have stayed put, what a dumbass.*

But the poem told deep things to my heart. I couldn't hide it. The others saw. They mocked me for liking the poem so much. For reciting it to myself under my breath.

A LONE SAILBOAT

I recited it before sleep.

I recited it when I made my body into a zodiac.

I recited it in prison.

ONE-TWO

Time erases people. Four walls. I forgot about everyone and maybe they forgot about me.

ONE-TWO

My ma passed away. Years increased. I'm not sure I spent them on earth. I didn't age the right way.

ONE-TWO

I became an afternoon with no crest into evening.
  I became another wall that kept myself in.
  I didn't care about anyone or anything.

THRICE

But then a great pain came to me. My stomach was vexed. Clouds filled the holes of my seeing.

THE STRANGER

She gave me one call to make.

AMERICA

I was outside, pacing around a streetlamp. Round and round. My shadow grew big and small. The phone rang and rang.
  You weren't picking up.

TEUTONIA AVENUE

I took the stairway, up six flights and pushed the heavy door. I walked up the hallway. My stomach was growling, because I was starving.
  I heard it over the growling. Your voice. Through the wall.

FIRE AND ICE

It's memory's sweat.

BAD BOY

What was I supposed to tell the *militzioner*?

That mathematics made me do it? That mathematics came to me and that the numbers braided themselves so beautifully and I just climbed the long lock of hair up, up, up to floor six?

IN EVERY DREAM NOW I'M CLIMBING THAT BRAID

It's ringing and ringing, but you won't pick up.

MY HEAD IS DRAINING

There. He's panting at my feet. Vaska. All muddy colors and sticky hair.

VASKA

He's bowing his nose. He's poking at my ankles. I'm ashamed.

VASKA!

Hefty, true.

He knows what I've done.

He knows what I'm about to do.

He knows what I keep doing.

NICKY?

Then you finally pick up.

TANYA, ALONE IN HER CELL

AND THE LORD SAID UNTO JOHN, COME FORTH AND YOU WILL RECEIVE ETERNAL LIFE

"But unfortunately, John came fifth…"

I PUNCH THE WALL

And laugh and laugh and laugh.

BECAUSE I LIKE PUNCHING AND LAUGHING

It makes me wet.

NOSTALGIA

Teenage night pimpled with stars.

SVETLANA

Teenage cunt stuffed with longing.

BESTIES

Sveta and I. We were at the mall. We had both just stolen some new bras from Victoria's Secret. We were on our way to the food court, cause Sveta wanted a fucking Cinnabon, even though she fucking knew that I was watching my figure. But what Sveta wants, Sveta gets.

As usual, I'm horny for no reason. As usual, I feel so ugly I can barely string my words together. As usual, I'm trying to be charming as fuck every other sentence, but as usual Sveta's attention is elsewhere.

WE GO WAY BACK, SVETA AND I
She's my bestie since elementary school.

HOW IT IS
Sometimes she makes me so wet. Sometimes my math homework makes me so wet. Sometimes the fucking sun rising on a new fucking day makes me so wet. What's a teenage cunt to do?

I'M A VIRGIN
I want to fuck morning, noon, and night.

SO WHAT
I want to fuck all the handles on all the doors.

JUST THERE
I love having my hand in my pants. Just to touch it.

RUMORS
I'm barely thirteen and some of the fucking fuckheads in our class sense that I'm horny and they make eyes at me. They pass me notes. They ask me to suck them off. To fuck them good. To sex them up. Whatever. Svetlana tells me people say I'm a gross hoe. I ask her if she wants to go down on me. She says, Ew, no! I jump on her and pin her hands to the floor. She says, Stop it, cut it out. I let go and say, Relax, Sveta, I'm not gonna fucking rape you. She laughs and pushes me off her and says, You're such a bitch, with her inching smile.

That night I masturbate to raping her.

FUCKHEADS OF HER DREAMS

There are always boys. We're fourteen, fifteen, sixteen, seventeen... And there are always boys.

CUTE BOYS

Sveta says, Hey, look over there. You see them? Who? Them. Who. The cute boys, duh. You gotta be fucking kidding me. Sveta with her sweet tits. Always looking for cute boys. Stocking up on cute boys as if we were in famine. Sveta likes all her cute boys. Here's the twist. Most of them aren't even cute. Like really not cute. She likes cute boys like strays like broken noses, like sadists like psychos, like scabs like sad hearts and sad dicks, it makes her feel like she's got a purpose in life. WHY DO WE ALL HAVE TO HAVE A FUCKING PURPOSE IN LIFE? The primordial lie.

She's pointing at them and smiling. She's so fucking obvious. Eating her gooey Cinnabon like a fucking bimbo. Of course, the two boys are looking at us now. They got mean eyes, those ones. I tell Sveta so. I say, Come on, Sveta, those two got mean eyes. She says, Nonsense, Tanyechka, they're cute! Let's call them over. Let's not, I say. No, let's, let's, let's, she's poking at my stomach and I hate her. I realize I'm completely wet. Why am I so fucking wet all the time?

The two boys with mean eyes get up and start to come over. One of them's sheepish and focused and kind of angelic if you think about it. The other one's only got one eye, and he's walking like he's been sent by God. My whole body's a bad feeling.

I get up and follow Sveta's lead.

DOSTOYEVSKY

We're at their house. The cute boys. The empty Bacardi bottle spins and spins and spins and lands on us. So I scooch up and Sveta scooches up and we kiss in front of the boys. Sveta acts shy. She's a fucking tease. She opens her eyes while she has her fucking tongue in my mouth and looks over at that fucking cyclops. I hope his fucking cock explodes. Svetlana is embarrassed by me. By my big mouth. I fucking hate her too. I'm glad, I'm glad, I'm glad we're both going to die.

CRIME AND PUNISHMENT

I don't know why I keep remembering this moment. It's fall. Before the bell for first period. I remember rushing to Sveta in the hall. She promised to give me her notes on *Crime and Punishment*. She hands me her notebook and I copy them super fucking quickly. I give them back and she smirks at me. Thanks, I say. You're welcome, she says. We smile at each other for a long fucking time.

LOVE

We are still in the hallway, smiling at each other, smiling, smiling, smiling, as our hair turns gray.

THE SONG I SING TO MYSELF IN PRISON

7-Eleven Big Gulp. My acrylic nails. Svetlana's eyes filled with my face. These are a few of my favorite things…

BOYFRIEND

Sveta would go gaga for him. Suburban white boy acting all thug-life.

Svetochka, I can still feel you smiling at me.

CRAZY MAMA

I told her I don't need a mama. Especially a crazy mama.

She's fucked up and dull as a spoon.

Sometimes I can't stop thinking about her.

Something like missing, something like needing, something like the blank soreness that comes after rage.

When she tells me a joke, I get these feelings.

I'm light-hearted and terrified, Crazy Mama.

CRAZY MAMA

MY DIMOCHKA

This is how it happened. I had just put more sun cream on my Dimochka. He wasn't like his friends, Apollos. He was white as a page. He burnt so easily. I had said, Dimochka, come here, let me put more sun cream on you. He said, Oh, Mama. He didn't want to leave the shore and his friends. But Dimochka was a good boy. He came to his mama. He didn't fuss about as I put the cream on. He let me be very thorough. Then of course he had to sit next to me to let it sink in. He didn't complain. His friends were rough-housing on the shore. Dima sat on his towel and poked his finger in the sand. I said, Dimochka, *zaichik*, what are you drawing in the sand? The figure had a curious form. A star, Mama, Dima said to me.

I followed the grooves in the sand.

I TRIED MY BEST TO RAISE HIM TO BE A GOOD PERSON

No one was religious back then. Religion had stopped with my parents, rest their souls.

I never, never showed Dimochka a star with six points. All the stars we drew together had five points. Normal stars. Safe stars.

I DIDN'T WANT TO DRAW ATTENTION TO IT

I replied in a half-voice, A star...

I kept my eyes on the sand, because I wasn't sure what emotion would happen if I lifted them.

STOICISM
Mercy.

A TRICK
To keep life going.

DIMOCHKA'S SUN CREAM HAD SOAKED INTO HIS PALE BODY
I rubbed the sand off my palms. You can go now, *moy khoroshinki*, I told him.

His little eyes grew cheerful. He waved to his friend and began running toward the shore.

When he was gone, I wiped the drawing from the sand.

I looked back up and took two deep breaths. There we go. My eyes focused on my Dimochka. He was splashing about with the other boys in a beautiful fury.

THE ORIGIN
I remember thinking how blessed he is that such a fury, in him, is a kind-natured one. If he were a mean-spirited boy, with such fury, he could destroy a whole world. (When I was pregnant with him, I often worried about this. What if my child is born with the wrong kind of fury?)

MAMA, MAMA
Then I heard him yelling my way from the shore.

MAMA, WE'RE GOING TO GO SWIMMING!
Such a good boy. He knew to ask me before going out into the water. I nodded and out he went.

MY GOOD BOY
Out he went, out into the water with a beautiful fury.

HIS PAPA
When my husband, Dimochka's father, passed away, Dima was two. I told myself, Oksana, you get yourself together. Oksana, you have a child to look after.

MY PARENTS
They had both passed when I was a little girl and left me and my older sister. It wasn't that uncommon. Or at least in our community. We couldn't complain. There were many orphans back then.

BY NATURE
I am not one who complains.

BUT THERE ARE THINGS THAT REMAIN PAINFUL
It's hard, still, to talk about my husband's departure. Forgive me if I cannot utter his name. He became, simply, Papa. To Dimochka he was Papa. To me, without Dimochka, he was no more. And so, at times, I talked about Papa. How Papa used to be. What Papa had looked like. How Dimochka looked like his Papa. Papa, yes, yes, yes. There would always be Papa. I had enough in me for that.

THE ACCIDENT
I don't want to describe the accident. It was an accident.

THE SEA
Yes, I still remember the sea. Remembering the sea is not impossible. At times, it is even its own body. Not the mass that took my Dimochka.

I DID NOT EXPERIENCE HATE
When my husband died. Perhaps I should have. Perhaps I somehow skipped over it. I know it is natural to experience it. But when my husband, Dimochka's Papa, left this world, I did not experience feelings akin to fire and ice. Maybe I am a fool. I don't know. I just accept what life gives me. I don't know how else to react.

FURY
The first thought I had, after the accident, was—I wish he had had the other fury,
    the mean fury
    not
    the beautiful fury
    I wish he would have destroyed this whole world.

LACUNA
That feeling left me.
    And for a long time, nothing took its place.

MY SISTER
Anya. She told me she would have taken that child, the one who had been in the water with him, the one who had swum by his side, the one who returned to shore without him, Anya said she would have taken that very child, and drown him in the same water.

THE OTHER BOY

I try to explain myself to Annechka with my utmost honesty. I'm ashamed that I do not hate that little boy for coming out of the water without my Dimochka. I'm ashamed that sometimes, in my sleeplessness, I am daydreaming about holding Dimochka, putting my nose in his hair, wrapping my arms around him, watching his eyelashes lift up and down when he looks around the room—and then suddenly, I realize I'm holding the other boy, the other one, that other boy—

TO SEE AND FEEL

I don't know why my head makes up things like this for me to see and feel. Over and over again. To see and feel. When it hurts. It hurts so much. To see and feel these things.

TOUCH

I tell Annechka. I tell her that I'm afraid. I'm afraid that I feel a sort of—*love*.

Love—that comes in waves.

Love—that fills me with light.

But the light inside me stings.

THAT'S IT

Anya says on the phone. You're coming here to live with us. What am I going to do in Moscow? I tell her. Anya laughs. There is so much to do in Moscow! Hell of a lot better than our little backward town. Why do you stick around there anyway? How can you bear it? To be in that apartment where Dimochka was. Oksanochka, *dorogaya*, you have to get out of there.

I KNOW WHAT I SOUND LIKE

I'm not sure if I can explain myself. I tried with Anya. I told her, I can't. I can't leave Dimochka.

I COULD HEAR HER SHIFTING THE RECEIVER AGAINST HER JAW

Oksanochka, she said firmly, Dima is gone.

He's gone.

He's gone, I agreed with her.

I said, Yes, Annechka, you're right.

He's gone.

SISTERS

My sister had made a good life for herself. She always knew how to go about things, make multitude out of very little. And she was a generous person, always. Ever since she was a little girl. But the knack that she had, I did not want. The things that she had, I did not want. She insisted and even pleaded. She came to visit (though she hated our little old town) and she said, I'm taking you back with me.

I kindly declined.

I TOOK HER HAND BETWEEN MY TWO PALMS

I said, Annechka, I am staying here and you are going back to Moscow. I kissed her on the cheek. She spotted Dima's small shoes, next to mine, by the door. She flinched at the sight of them.

She asked me, in a very soft voice, if I wanted help putting them away.

I told her that I did not want her help putting them away, but thank you.

She told me, more firmly, that it's time to put those things away.

I told her, more firmly, that I cannot do that.

She told me, more firmly, that I have to try.

I told her, more firmly, that I am trying.

She told me, more firmly, that I have to *want* to survive.

BEFORE SHE LEFT

Anya held me by my arms and slipped quite a lot of bills into my apron pocket. I tried to refuse, but she said, Please, Oksanochka, just take it. I thanked her and said goodbye.

IN HER ABSENCE

The apartment was quiet again. I took the bills out, a considerable sum. I was happy to see how well she was doing, if she was leaving this for me.

THE NEXT MORNING

I went downstairs to floor five. There were two families there with small children. I gave half of it to the Bokuchavas and the other half the Neschastlivyis. They looked at me with wonder and with pity. But they took the money.

I closed the door behind me, took off my shoes, and placed them next to Dima's.

DAYS LATER, FOOTSTEPS

Small ones. Going up the stairs. When I heard them, I naturally got up from the kitchen table where I had been sifting the bad buckwheat seeds out of the pot I intended to cook that evening. I naturally went to the door.

How burdened a young boy's footsteps can be.

THRESHOLD
I naturally went to the door. Naturally, I turned the knob and—
for a second I was in between two worlds, I think.

There was a boy, standing, at the threshold. He was looking
up at me. It was not my Dima.

NICKY, NICKY,
Little Nicky from floor five.

THERE WAS A STORM IN HIS EYES
And I followed it.

He began to lift the kitchen knife that he was holding.

NICKY, NICKY, NIKOLAI
I took a step forward.

IN THE BEGINNING
There was the word, and the word was Yes, and I said it three
times.

SALLY

YES, YES, YES
But no more Motherhood.

SOME SAY
God brings us here and God guides us back. It was not God who came to me and took me elsewhere.

IT WAS A YOUNG WOMAN, ACTUALLY
With caramel skin and the most perfectly drawn cupid's bow to her lip I have ever seen.

SALLY
She said to me.

 I came to in a bathtub. I was very cold and wet.

 My name would henceforth be Sally, she explained.

 Repeat after me, Sally. Sally. Sally.

 I don't want a new life, I wheezed.

 She took my thumb and my forefinger and pressed them together.

 Un, deux, trois... My mouth filled with water.

OPEN SEA
Sally. Sally. Sally. I sailed.

 I felt so alone that my skin could have peeled off with the wind.

S

I am sipping a cold strawberry-flavored ice cream from a straw. Around me, it smells like fried potatoes.

A

What is it that the Greeks tried to teach us? Loss may be our only fortune?

L

I open my mouth. What a gentle Anglo-Saxon tone. I ask the waitress for a serving of fries. She brings me a plate of fries.

"Careful," she says, "they're hot."

I pick one up carefully with my thumb and my forefinger. I dip it into my cold cup of ice cream.

Fire and ice.

"I like eating them that way too," a man says to me, twisting his baseball cap deeper onto his head.

I don't understand what is metaphor and what isn't.

I pull the sleeves up on my cardigan. It's so soft. I can't stop touching the rosy pink weaving.

L

The waitress tells me to call her Lisette.

Y

"Sally…" Lisette is calling my attention.

I look up. "Yes?"

"The most important thing is," Lisette says as she leans over the counter, "that now…" she leans in even closer and whispers, "you're with us."

US

It's not what I would have expected. There are no angels. No apostles. No saints. There is only *Cosa Nostra*.

"This is your home, now," Lisette explains.

I dip a French fry into the cloud of whipped cream atop my new ice cream drink.

EXERCISES

Lisette tells me we have to do regular exercises to help my mind stay on this side of the story.

EXERCISE WITH THE PHOTO

Lisette shows me a photo and asks me who this is.

"This is little Nicky from floor five," I reply.

"Good," Lisette says. "And who is Nicky?"

"He's the one who killed me."

"Correct," Lisette says. There is a fine dip in her lip and I like to stare at it. Lisette taps the photo to get my attention.

"Sally," she says.

"Yes." I look back at the photo.

GENERAL QUESTIONS

"Sally, are you in pain?"

I take a moment to reflect.

"I don't know," I respond.

"Do you remember what pain feels like?"

I take a moment to reflect.

"I suppose it's unpleasant."

"That's right. And…?"

"And…" I'm concentrating, "it preoccupies the psyche at large."

"And?"

"And…" I keep thinking, "it feels very personal."

Lisette refills my glass of water, and the ice cubes crackle.

SPECIFICS

"Can you remember the last time you felt pain?"

I think about it carefully and I see no evidence to share. I shake my head.

IMAGINATION EXERCISE

"Close your eyes," Lisette says, "and I want you to imagine the sea and the waves coming toward you. Do you see it?"

I close my eyes. I can feel Lisette's hand on my own hand, resting on the counter. She is softly pressing my thumb and forefinger together, so that they touch and separate, touch and separate. I hear the waves, squeezing, curling, rushing forward.

"I see the water," I tell her.

"What do you feel," Lisette asks quietly.

I shrug.

"Nothing."

Now both of my hands are being guided by Lisette. Touching and separating. Touching and separating.

"Can you see a little boy on the shore?" she asks.

IMAGINATION EXERCISE REVISITED

There is a little boy, pattering his feet in the sea foam on the shore.

"Yes," I say, "I see him."

"What do you feel?" she asks.

I shrug. "Nothing," I say.

"Keep watching," she whispers.

The little boy runs into the water. He starts swimming.

IMAGINATION EXERCISE REVISITED

There's a little boy out in the water. I see his head bobbing up and down. The waves are getting bigger. There is another boy. Their arms are twining together.

IMAGINATION EXERCISE REVISITED

There is a little boy out near the horizon. He is all alone.

"Do you see his face?"

"Yes."

"And?"

"I think he would like to get out of the water."

"Why doesn't he?"

"I think the water wants him to stay in."

IMAGINATION EXERCISE REVISITED

There is a little boy being sucked into the water.

"Sally?" Lisette whispers.

"Yes?"

"If you feel nothing," she asks, "then what's coming out of your eyes?"

JOKEBOOK

Lisette has given me a book of jokes. She encourages me to memorize them. It's important to have a sense of humor about my situation. I memorize the jokes.

TANYA

Lisette tells me to visit a girl named Tanya and tell her my jokes. The girl named Tanya lives in a room with one wall made of bars. When the guard opens the bars, I step inside her room. Tanya tells me to get the fuck out. Tanya tries to scratch up my face. The guard hits her knuckles with the baton.

TANYA TELLS ME THAT I'M A CRAZY MAMA

She has strong opinions. She has a willful sense of character. Tanya tells me I'm the most pathetic old hag she's ever seen. I tell her I don't understand what she means. Tanya tells me that she's seen my boy. My boy? Yeah, Mama, your fucking kid. I don't have a child. Yeah you fucking do, Tanya says. I smile and shake my head. Tanya grabs my head with her two swollen hands. Wake up, Crazy Mama, she screams into my face.

IT'S OKAY

I tell her that she has a difficult character, but it does not bother me.

She tells me if I show my fucking face in her cell again she'll pull my eyeballs out with her fingers and stuff them up my asshole.

I ask her if she wants to hear a joke.

WHAT DID ONE MURDERER SAY TO THE OTHER?

Tanya waits for the punchline like a child.

Tanya is a child.

Tanya wants to punch each line out of my mouth.

Tanya wants a good laugh so she can be a good girl.

"Knife to meet you."

WHEN SHE LAUGHS

There's a sinking feeling. A drain in my heart gulping up her voice. It feels dirty and thick.

I don't know why, but when it's gone, I miss it.

I tell Lisette so.

RUSSIAN DOLLS

"They are unbearable, aren't they?" I say to Tanya.

"Oh yeah?" Her eyes light up.

"Well," I continue, "they are just so full of themselves…"

MY CHEST

Feels like it's leaking.

ONE MORE, CRAZY MAMA!

"All right just one more," I tell her.

"Tell me the Jewish one again, that's a fucking good one."

The word "Jewish" takes my breath away.

"Crazy Mama?" Tanya asks.

There's sand on my tongue.

THE JEWISH ONE

"How do you know a Jew is mad at you?" I ask Tanya.

"How, how, how??" she's jumping up and down.

"They tell you to Go to Hell… and then worry that you'll get there all right."

A SMALL FINGER

Inching its way on my tongue like a caterpillar. Pulling itself down my throat.

I vomit into the steel toilet.

"Shit, Crazy Mama, that's fucking gross!" Tanya yells out.

EVERYONE HAS A PURPOSE IN LIFE

That's what Lisette tells me to tell Tanya.

"What's my purpose then, if you're such a smart ass?" Tanya says.

VISITOR

Tanya likes games. Lisette says that's very useful. She tells me to tell her that she's going to have a visitor. Tanya can teach him a lesson. Tanya can take her time with it. It keeps Tanya occupied.

"Those who cannot find peace," Lisette says, "should be kept occupied."

WHAT'S IN IT FOR ME?

Tanya asks.

"Well," I tell her, "they told me they'll let you get your nails done regularly."

"For real?"

"And…"

"And?"

"And you can do whatever you want with him. I heard you have very strong hands, Tanyechka."

THE SEA

Every now and then, the sea still comes to my eyes.

I report this to Lisette.

LISETTE TEACHES ME SOMETHING IN HER LANGUAGE

I repeat it diligently. She tells me my accent is not too bad. I try to improve it. I would like to say it just like her. I repeat it in the morning and I repeat it at night. Lisette tells me that it is sounding better and better.

Cet amour, cet amour, cet amour,
This love,

THIS LOVE

When I sleep, I dream of waves, sparkling waves, that burn, burn, burn with the same voice.

I am

a   lone

sailboat

sailboat

sailboat

sailboat

sailboat

sailboat

sailboat

sailboat

sailboat

sailboat

sailboat

sailboat

sailboat

mama come look I'm sparkling mama look look I sparkle mama don't come near me it will sizzle mama stay away mama I miss you mama where are you mama show yourself come closer mama step back mama my tears cry tears cry tears cry tears for you mama I burn I will burn you mama if you hold me hold me hold me hold me hold me mama don't come any closer the world will end it will end it will end mama with my touch

BROTHERS

MY SISTER, LISETTE

She's kind of like my best friend. She's kind of like my mom. She's kind of like my home.

THE FUTURE

My sister, Lisette, has always attracted people to her. They just come to her. They ask her questions. Whenever we go anywhere, the whole place gathers around her. Asking her questions. Questions about the future.

TRICKS

My sister, Lisette, has tricks she teaches people sometimes. Tricks to help them. People want to be helped. But then, they get angry at Lisette when it hurts.

HER CUPID'S BOW

My sister, Lisette, never forces anyone. People just listen to her. When we're all alone, she tells me that it's funny—the choice— people think—they have.

I MET THIS JEWISH BOY

I tell my sister. He's really nice. She asks me where I met him. I say on the street. Where on the street, she asks. I say on the street, on the street. Like he's got no home? She asks. I nod.

BROTHERS

I'm so happy cause I always wanted a brother. I don't tell my sister that. I don't want her to feel bad, or like she's not enough. It's different. Brothers.

AT FIRST WE MAKE HIM A BED OUT OF BLANKETS NEXT TO MY BED

He sleeps there. I never ask him anything about his one bad eye. I know you're not supposed to bring that type of stuff up to people. Instead, I ask him about his necklace. He lets me touch it. Says he found it. In the sand. Where? I ask. Near Lake Michigan? No, he says, in the sand in the Soviet Union. Oh yeah? I say. I'm not sure where the Soviet Union is. He can see that. He says, It was east. But that it doesn't exist anymore. He holds the pendant between his fingertips and he tells me it's the only thing of value in his life.

Soon, he just sleeps with me in my bed.

SUNRISE, SUNSET

On Friday at sundown, he says he can't touch anything with electricity. He asks me to turn on and off the lights for him. He asks me not to heat up his food for him. He tells me he faces east to pray. In the direction of the beach where he found his necklace. And when he prays it sounds like singing. And when he sings, he's probably the most beautiful human I have ever seen.

TROUBLE

I got to study during the day, because I'm still finishing up my high school degree.

Cause I messed up last year at school. Cause I got into trouble. What kind of trouble? he asks me. I don't wanna say.

He puts his hand on my wrist and tells me it's okay. I don't have to say if I don't want to. I look down at the carpet. I just stopped going to school, I guess. You gotta show up, apparently, I say. He laughs. Then when it's quiet again, I tell him that sometimes I get really afraid. For no reason. I don't know why. Something'll just make me really afraid. And then I'm scared. I'm so scared.

HE TELLS ME
He understands.

THAT NIGHT
He asks me if I'm sleeping. I say no. He twists and turns on his side. Then he stops. He lies on his back and stares at the ceiling. I do the same. We forgot to close the curtain, so there's a little bit of moon running across our knees. Otherwise it's dark. He tells me that he loves me. I tell him that I love him too.

LOVE
After that, I realize there is a word in my heart. And that word is his name. And his name is my shelter. And I say it three times. For luck. For safety. For warmth.

M
I tell him he shouldn't be shy, if he's hungry he needs to go to the diner on 79th and Capitol and Lisette can get him whatever he wants to eat there. He tells me he can only eat things prepared in such and such a way. I tell him Lisette can prepare it any way he wants. He tells me that he is ashamed that for years, he did not abide by the rules that God has asked him to follow. I tell him surely God would understand if he needed to bend the rules a bit when he was homeless. He says he's lucky that now he has a home.

O

He tells me he's got a sister, but not like mine. I want to know— her age, her name, the color of her hair. All this information from his life is like a pencil drawing him with more and more lines. I want to know, do they have similar ears? I want to know, does she also have a problem with her eye? I want to know, would I love her as deeply as I love him?

He asks me never to ask anything else about that family again.

S

"You're my family now," he says.

H

Lisette puts her arms around us both and asks how she got so lucky to have two brothers like us. My chest is full of my own breath. I see him with his one eye wet with tears.

Lisette calls us Her Boys.

I study with all my might (and with lots of his help) and I get my GED!

E

It's summer again and I am loved.

We both get jobs cleaning the YMCA northwest of Brown Deer. Sometimes we even get the same shift. He dances with the mop. I make dinosaur noises in my big yellow latex disinfecting gloves.

FEET

His white Nikes are almost completely yellow. I tell him I can clean them up for him if he'd like. He says he'd like that very much. I clean each shoe very carefully, using a rag and the soft pad of my finger and my nail to get into the stitching. When I'm done, they are white as white. He says, Thank you, many times, and I say, You're welcome, many times, until it becomes another game we play.

MY BOYS
Lisette tells us how proud she is of us. It's already autumn, but I got a good tan in. He tells me how handsome I am with my tan. I tell him he's the most beautiful one-eyed ghost I've ever seen.

We touch mouths. Then lips. Then tongues.

He wraps his arms tightly around my back and I do the same. I can feel his shoulder blades underneath my spread palms. I bury my head in his neck and he pushes his ear into my shoulder. His heart is beating so fast, as if frantically knocking on the door of my chest.

OFTEN
We are swans together.

THE GIFT
One morning, he unhooks his necklace and puts it around my neck. He tells me he wants me to have it. I tell him I can't, I really can't accept it. He says, Please, keep it safe for me. What do you mean, safe? I ask.

SHE'S GOT HER BELLY BUTTON PIERCED
With a dangling jewel. She almost always shows it off with a cropped shirt or sweat-shirt or sweater, or sometimes she just rolls her T-shirt up so it sticks out. Her best friend's got long auburn hair she lets slide over her shoulder. She looks angry and heart-broken at the same time.

WE SEE THEM WHEN WE GO TO THE MALL
So we start to follow them.

IN THE BATHROOM STALL
I say his name once for luck. Once for safety. Once for warmth.

HE POINTS THEM OUT TO ME
"There they are," he says. We follow them up the escalator. We wait outside of Victoria's Secret.

They walk out as if they're holding in a laugh, they walk briskly. They stop at the fountain. They poke at each other with wide smiles. We wait. They go to the food court. We walk behind them. They stand in line at the Cinnabon. We sit at a table and watch them. They sit at a different table. The blond one looks over at us. She has a smile that's sweet and psychotic at the same time. I don't trust her. I tell him, I'm scared. He tells me not to worry, because he will always take care of me. I look into his eye and I feel calm and repetitive.

He tells me to look back at the blond and smile shy the way I smile shy. I am shy. I don't like to talk to people I don't know. And I don't like to talk to girls I don't know. And I don't want to talk to anyone, except for him. And my sister, Lisette.

But I smile shy at the blond. And then he says, Smile like that at the brunette. So I smile shy at the brunette one too. She looks back at me tightly. I think she's angry with me. But I'm not sure why. Maybe I'm the one who is angry? Sometimes it's hard to tell the difference between what you feel and what someone else feels.

HE TAKES MY HAND UNDER THE TABLE
I'm not going to let anything happen to you, he tells me. Then

118

he gets up and I get up with him and we start walking over to the girls.

WE'RE STANDING AND THEY ARE SITTING
"I'm Sveta," the blond one says, "and this is my bestie, Tanya. What are your names?"

"I'm Moshe," he says, "and this is my brother Rémy."

"That's funny," Sveta says. "He doesn't look like your brother. He's too Brown. Plus you only got one eye."

Then she puts her hand over her mouth.

"Oh I didn't mean it like that! It looks cute on you, the one eye!"

"Why, thanks," Moshe says, and he smiles at both of them.

MY HANDS ARE IN MY POCKETS
"Wanna come over to our place," he says to them.

THEY FOLLOW US
As we walk all the way back to our home.

I'm keeping my eyes to the cement, counting the curbs we pass.

The girls are pulling at each other's shirts and pinching each other's shoulders. I think one of them is trying to play a game.

WE UNLOCK THE DOOR AND TAKE OFF OUR SHOES AND GO UP TO OUR BEDROOM
Lisette's at work. I sit down on the carpet with the two girls.

"You got anything to drink or what," Tanya says.

"Sure we do." He goes downstairs and comes back up with a half-bottle of Bacardi.

We take gulps one by one. It sounds like when flowers want to pop open for spring.

SPEAK UP

Tanya says to me. Apparently I'm speaking softly. I swallow and pinch my lips with my teeth.

"Your brother or whatever is fucking awkward," Tanya says to him.

HOW ABOUT

"We play spin the bottle!" Sveta says with her eyes glittering.

"Great idea," he tells her, "let's finish the bottle."

Sveta chugs the liquid down.

Tanya's looking at me with disgust. I ask her, quietly, if she's feeling all right.

"I'm feeling fucking wonderful, just wonderful!" she says through a tense jaw.

THE BOTTLE SPINS AND SPINS AND SPINS

It lands on me and Sveta.

I keep my eyes to the carpet. Sveta inches closer to me while she pulls up her low-waist jeans.

"Go on, don't be scared," she says to me softly.

I raise my eyes and glide them over to her.

"You'll see," he says to Sveta, "Rémy's a great kisser."

HER EYES BRIGHTEN

"Oh yeah?" Sveta says.

READY

There is a shadow across my lips. It's the outline of Sveta's face, with the sun coming in from the window where we forgot to close the curtains again.

She replaces the shadow with her lips.

I can feel her tongue wiggling against my teeth.

I open my mouth and let her in.

Her tongue is caressing my taste buds and it feels okay.

"That's enough for now," he says and takes Sveta's shoulder and pulls her away from me.

ONE-TWO

Sveta spins the bottle now. It lands on her and Tanya.

The girls smile at each other and suddenly Tanya looks powerful and warm. They lean into each other. I see their tongues jump in and out of each other's mouths like fish.

Sveta pulls away and Tanya licks her lips.

IT'S TANYA'S TURN

She spins the bottle and it lands on him.

I knew it would land on him.

GREAT, I HAVE TO KISS THE FUCKING CYCLOPS NOW

Tanya says.

"I don't want to see your fucking boner, by the way, so if you're gonna get hard off this, I'll vomit in your mouth, fair warning."

"Don't worry," he says, "I won't get hard."

Sveta laughs and says, "I mean, you can get a little hard…"

Tanya slaps her in the gut.

Sveta turns to Tanya and gives her a big pout.

"Don't be no-fun, Tanyechka, please…"

"All right, let's just fucking make out."

TANYA SCOOCHES OVER TO HIM

She leans into his face and puts her mouth up against his. I see her lips open and her tongue slide into his mouth. I don't see his tongue. Maybe he keeps it to himself.

ON HIS LAP

There's Sveta's hand, caressing his thigh. She's moving her palm over to his crotch and scrunching her fingers over his zipper.

"Come on," Sveta is whispering, "don't be shy now, I want to feel it get firm."

Tanya pulls back and looks at Sveta's hand. She slaps it away.

"You fucking hoe, I swear to God, you're such a fucking skank I can't even."

"Ouch!" Sveta whimpers. "What, I wanna feel his bulge, don't be jealous."

"I'm not fucking jealous, I'm fucking humiliated."

"Ugh, you're such a drag, you know that."

"You're the one with a stank-ass drip in your shop-lifted panties for any defunct *cutie* with a floppy something between his legs and—"

"Excuse me! Tanya, everyone knows you're a dyke and that you're in love with me and you know what, I'm tired of standing up for you all the time, cause you know what, you are a dyke and you are in love with me—"

TANYA SLAPS SVETA HARD IN THE FACE

The whole room freezes.

SVETA TOUCHES HER CHEEK

"You... fucking... *suka*..." Sveta says quietly.

"What?" Tanya says, "did I embarrass you in front of the *cute boys*?"

SVETA JUMPS ON TOP OF TANYA

She's clawing at her face. Tanya is holding her back by the wrists.

"*Davai*, Sveta, you want to charm these *svolachi*, go ahead and charm them!"

"They're not *svolachi*, they're nice boys!"

"Nice boys? Says the *shlyukha*!"

YOU'RE THE FUCKING *SHLYUKHA*

Sveta spits at Tanya's face. It lands on the side of her nose. Tanya pushes her off with one loud grunt. Sveta falls back. Tanya lunges at her. Sveta pulls her legs into herself then juts them out. One shoe gets Tanya in the gut. She heaves, then flings her arms out.

TANYA HAS SVETA BY THE THROAT

I look away. I am worried.

"Get... off...!"

Sveta is choking.

Sveta is gagging.

SVETA IS GASPING FOR AIR

Tanya pushes her down on the ground and gets on top of her.

I look at him. He is sitting very still. He is doing nothing. I try to do what he is doing.

TANYA LETS GO OF HER THROAT

Sveta is breathing like a bullfrog.

"*Nu shto...*" Tanya whispers into her ear. *Well now.*

Sveta presses her teeth together.

I cover my eyes with my hands.

WHEN I OPEN THEM

The girls are on top of each other.

The girls are rubbing against each other's bodies.

Sveta's hands are in Tanya's hair by the fistfuls.

Tanya is gripping onto Sveta's back.

I FUCKING HATE YOU

Tanya is gritting into her best friend's face.

I HATE YOU MORE

Sveta huffs right back at her, then slaps her hand on Tanya's butt and squeezes the flesh there.

THE GIRLS ARE SO ANGRY BUT ALSO SOMETHING ELSE

"Fuck you," Tanya says through her clenched teeth.

Sveta closes her eyes as she moans.

"You're a fucking skank," Tanya exhales.

Sveta opens her eyes. "You're the dirty hoe," she whispers.

The girls start licking each other's faces.

"I'm so wet," Tanya grits, "and it's your fucking fault."

They start tonguing each other and pushing and pulling to-and-fro.

Sveta clamps down onto Tanya. Tanya wraps her arms around Sveta. They're holding each other so tightly.

Tanya lets her legs fall open and Sveta starts rubbing her pelvis between them.

I decide to look down at the carpet.

When I look back up, he is standing. He is holding a knife.

THAT'S THE KNIFE FROM THE KITCHEN, I SAY

The girls stop what they're doing. There is saliva and bite marks all over their faces.

"Hey," Sveta asks him from underneath Tanya. "What are you going to do with that?"

HIS BLUE EYE LOOKS COMPLETELY EMPTY

"Moshe?" I say.

He's shaking his head.

THE GIRLS ARE UP ON THEIR FEET

"Woa, woa…" Tanya is saying.

SVETA HAS HER BACK AGAINST THE DOOR

She's trying to turn the doorknob with her hand twisted behind her.

HEY, WHY'S YOUR DOOR LOCKED?

Sveta says.

I don't know where to look.

Tanya starts laughing and her voice is so loud.

I KNEW IT

"I knew they were gonna fucking kill us!" Tanya says, "You're gonna fucking kill us, aren't you?"

CUT IT OUT

Sveta says. She's trying the door again.

THE DOOR IS LOCKED
He says.
  The knife is still at his hip.

ARE YOU REALLY GONNA KILL US?
Sveta swallows.
  "Duh!" Tanya yells out. "What do you expect, your cute boys are a pair of psychos, Sveta, *durochka!*"

OH NO
Sveta makes an O with her mouth. Her eyes are silky.
  "Oh," she says.
  "Oh," she repeats.
  Sveta undoes the button of her jeans and slowly pulls her zipper down.
  "If that's what you wanted, you could have just said so, Moshe, you already know I have a super crush on you."
  He shakes his head. "It's Misha."

WAIT
Sveta chirps out. Her voice is getting higher and brittle.
  "I'll do whatever you want, honestly I will, whatever you want, I'm really good at it, you know, at all the things that you want, I'm really good and I actually like doing it, so whatever it is you want, I also really want to do that with you."
  "I don't want that," he says.

HE GRIPS THE KNIFE
Both of the girls start screaming.

I REACH OUT TO TOUCH HIS SHOULDER
He looks down at my hand. Then at my face.
"It's me. It's your brother," I say.
"My brother?"
He tilts his head.
"I don't have a brother," he tells me.

WHO WANTS TO GO FIRST?
He asks the girls.

MOSHE, STOP
I say.

HE PUSHES ME AWAY
My back hits the wall.

THE DOORKNOB IS RATTLING IN THE DOOR
The girls are trying to break it.

PLEASE, MOSHE, PLEASE
"Get away from me!" he barks.
He sounds just like a dog. An angry dog.
I'm scared.

THE FIRST JUT GOES INTO HER STOMACH
There's blood leaking down Tanya's jeans.
Sveta is trying to break the window to get out.

THE SECOND JUT GOES INTO HER ABDOMEN

Tanya is hacking up blood. Tanya looks down. She is staring at her own wounds with total vacancy.

THE THIRD JUT GOES INTO HER CHEST

Tanya lets out a dry choke. It's weird. It's almost a laugh.

She stumbles back and falls down onto the bed with her arms open like an angel.

Sveta faints.

M

The necklace is ice cold around my neck.

O

"Why are you crying," he yells at me.

S

I'm crouching against the wall. The wall that faces east.

H

I'm sweating. I'm ice cold.

E

I tap my thumb to my finger. *Un, deux, trois. Un, deux, trois.* But I'm still here.

GET UP

He barks at me again.

"And help me."

I DON'T WANT TO HELP YOU
I whimper.

He points the knife at me.

I'm scared and confused.

"Are you gonna kill me too, Moshe?" I murmur.

"*Moshe*," he says to himself and squints. "*Moshe, Moshe...*"

He squints and squints and squints.

He turns away from me. He walks toward Sveta's body by the window.

THERE IS BLOOD EVERYWHERE
In my room. Where I sleep. In our room. Where we sleep.

HE WIPES HIS HANDS ON HIS TORSO
Leaving bright red streaks across his chest.

THE DAY IS FALLING
The curtain is not fully drawn.

The light from the window cuts the room in half.

OH NO
The knife is in my hand.

OH NO
The knife is in Svetlana's chest.

OH NO
Three holes, leaking.

BROTHER?

I drop the knife and he drops to his knees. Ouch. I'm afraid he's cracked his knees.

I'M WIDE AWAKE

He's yelling at me. His voice is high and nervous. He sounds like a baby pig. No, he sounds like a little boy.

RÉMY

"We have to put them in the tub."

BROTHERS

I take the feet, he takes the under-arms. We haul their bodies to the bathroom one by one. We fold them into each other in the tub. He tells me to run the water cold. I run the water cold. It fills their toes and their folded legs and rises up to their hips. Their heads are flopped over their knees. The water takes their hair and makes it soppy and coinciding.

MY HANDS ARE IN THE COLD WATER

His hands are in the cold water too.

He tries to intertwine his fingers into mine. A sinking boat.

SEPULCHER

Your eyes are cold. Let me.

Your lips are cold. Let me.

Your heart is cold. Let me.

The water is cold.

MY HAND SLIPS OUT OF HIS HAND

I take my hand out of the water.

"You did something bad," I tell him.

His blue eye squeezes. It looks like it's going to break.

"So did you..."

HIS TWO HANDS

They are fishing about in the tub. He is braiding Tanya's hair into Sveta's hair. Dark into light. Tangled, wet threads.

WHY, I ASK, WHY, WHY, I ASK, WHY, WHY, I ASK, WHY

Un, deux, trois.

THERE IS A KNOCK ON THE DOOR

When he stands up, the water rolls down his fingers and drips onto the floor.

My throat is empty. I'm touching my collarbone.

The water is flooding over the sides of the tub, spilling across the floor, running up to the shoes of the man in the leather jacket and Brewers hat standing in the doorway.

THE BATHTUB

DRIP
Sveta.

DRIP
Hey, Sveta.
Sveta.
It's me.

DRIP, DRIP
It's your bestie, Tanya.

HELLO, HELLO, HELLO
You up?
Whatchya doing?
Do you wanna punish me?

A LITTLE SAILBOAT
Sveta.
Hey, Sveta.
Look our hair's all tangled and wet!

SVETA
You dead?

WHO'S GONNA PUNISH ME?
I'm a gross bitch.

YOU SAID YOU'D HELP ME WITH SCHOOL
Gulp, gulp, look at all this water.

TRUTH OR DARE
I kind of liked it when he stabbed me.
    It made me feel close to you.

OKAY, I'M A DYKE
You happy?
    I'm blowing you bubbles under the water.
    They're secret messages!

I'M SORRY ABOUT WHAT I SAID EARLIER
About you being a skank and everything.

ARE YOU SORRY ABOUT WHAT YOU SAID TO ME TOO?
Bubble, bubble.

COME ON, WAKE UP
We have to go over *Crime and Punishment*, remember?

WHAT DID DOSTOYEVSKY MEAN
When he wrote,
    "To go wrong in one's own way is better than to go right in someone else's."

BUBBLE, BUBBLE
Why don't you wake up like me?

AMERICA SUCKS
Right?
   Let's go somewhere else together.
   Me and You.

LADIES AND GENTLEMEN
This world is sad, Sveta, and every day I wake up half-dead already and in my dumb-dumb cadaver I still want to laugh so bad it hurts, it hurts.

WHAT DID DOSTOYEVSKY MEAN
When he wrote,
   "The darker the night, the brighter the stars,
   The deeper the grief, the closer is God!"

TRUTH
I'm in love with you, Svetlana.

EVERYTHING IS WORTHLESS
But I think you're beautiful.

GUESS WHAT?
I smell like lilacs.
   I smell like lollipops.
   I smell like death.

I KNOW, I KNOW
I'm not capable of love.

I WANT TO HEAR YOU LAUGH
Aren't I your favorite joke?
Come on, laugh at me, Sveta.

SO I HAVE AN OBSESSIVE PERSONALITY
I'm a broken record.
But I'm your broken record.

SVETA
Nothing is literal.

BUBBLE, BUBBLE
Death is a spell.

I NEED YOU
Wake up.

PLEASE
I'm failing at school.

DOUBLE PLEASE
I'm failing at life.

TRIPLE PLEASE
My lungs are failing.

TRUTH
I don't want to die I don't want to die I don't want to die I don't
want to die I don't want to die I don't want to die I don't want
to die I don't want to die I don't want to die I don't want to die
I don't want to die I don't want to die I don't want to die I don't
want to die…

DARE
Are you close to God?

TEUTONIA AVENUE

KNOCK, KNOCK
"It's me, Nicky."

I'M PACING AT THE CORNER
At the stop sign. It's dark everywhere, except for the low light that the moon gives.

I'M RUNNING THE NECKLACE FROM ONE PALM TO THE OTHER
Like a stream of water.

YO, HOMIE!
A kid yells out in my direction.

YO, OVER HERE, MAN!
He's across the street. His face is in the shadow. He's got big shorts, wide and loopy. His T-shirt bunched. His zip-up sweatshirt gaping open.

ONE-TWO
I lean away from him and feign a cough. I put the necklace in my mouth, under my tongue. I straighten back up.

YOU OKAY, HOMIE?
The kid takes a step into the street. He lifts his T-shirt. There's a

bit of his skinny white belly. There's a black fist tucked into his underwear. It's a gun.

I RAISE MY ARMS INTO THE AIR AND LOWER MYSELF ONTO MY KNEES

A reflex, slow and focused. I lower my chin and make sure not to look at him. A ruffle of wind.

RELAX, HOMIE

"I ain't gonna shoot you," he says, coming closer.

I keep my eyes to the sidewalk.

THE SONG OF BRUTUS

Authority is so lyrical. Our music, *Bozhé*.

I HAVE BEEN PUNISHED SO MANY TIMES

Punishment means very little to me. But as a man of the system, I have an ear for its music.

GET UP

The kid tells me.

I GET UP TO MY FEET

He flicks his head at me. I know to lower my arms.

I keep my palms facing toward him just in case. I wait for further instructions.

A TRICK I LEARNED IN PRISON

The American kid says he's been watching me. I slide the necklace discreetly behind my gums with my tongue.

LOOK AT ME IN THE EYES

He says.

I like it when the instructions are clear.

I look at him in the eyes.

SOMETIMES I'M SO TIRED OF HAVING TO EXPLAIN EVERYTHING

The kid tells me.

"You feel me, homie?"

I nod my head yes.

The kid's pulling his tongue out, just to stretch it. He looks both ways. Then smiles.

"You got something I want," he says.

I USED TO BE AFRAID TO DIE

I was just a kid.

I was never a kid.

I was fourteen.

There are boys and there are men and there are criminals.

IT'S NOT EASY TO CRY

For nobody. Even a baby has got to use all the force in its little body when it wails. It's got to shake and quake and shimmer and go red in the face with tears and snot. It's got no choice. This is how we ask to stay alive.

It's not easy to ask for life. Not for girls and not for boys and not for women and not for men, and not for nobody who was birthed and left asking.

CRIMINALS CRY

Scarred-up mammoths and lanky loners and seedy Samsons. All

razor-bald and stiff-eyed and reeking of abandon. Proud and fatherless, sanctimonious barbarians, rattled prey.

IN PRISON

I don't know why my life began to matter just then. I began asking for life.

THIS IS HOW

I became a little songbird with no song to sing. That's what the other men told me. That I was a little bird. When they took turns with their fists in my gut. In the beginning.

I don't want to go into the details. Their force. Their reign.

They were owed a song.

I owed them a song.

And I sang it, I sang it.

Until my fear went away. I'm not sure where. But it flew from me. Away.

NOW WHEN I'M AWAKE

I'm no longer afraid to die.

BUT IN MY SLEEP

I'm still afraid. In my sleep, I'm so angry with myself. In my sleep, I'm a little boy and I can't grow up. In my sleep, I'm a murderer. In my sleep, there is a dog that is smelling me, and a baby that is spitting out my soul with disgust.

I KEEP MY MOUTH SHUT

"Well, well," the kid says. "Looks like we got a hero."

He tells me to get back down on my knees.

He lifts his shirt and pulls his gun out of his waistband and points it at my temple.

THE STREET IS SILENT
So am I.

HE PUSHES THE NOSE OF THE GUN INTO MY SKIN SO I FEEL IT
"I'm waiting…" he says.

I LOOSEN MY JAW, CAREFUL TO KEEP THE NECKLACE IN PLACE
"Tweet, tweet," I make a bird sound through my closed lips.

HE LEANS DOWN TO MY FACE
"What the fuck did you just say?"
    "Tweet, tweet…" I repeat it.

DON'T LOOK AT THE FUCKING GROUND, LOOK AT ME WHEN I'M TALKING TO YOU
I lift my eyes.

REPEAT WHAT YOU JUST SAID TO ME, YOU OLD FAGGOT
"Tweet, tweet…" I sing again.

YOU BITCH ASS BITCH
"Tweet, tweet…" I chirp through my lips.

YOU THINK YOU BEING FUNNY, YOU LITTLE FUCK

I'm singing for him.

    Tweet, tweet.

    Tweet, tweet

    Goes my song—

WHEN HE

Pulls the trigger.

THE LAST SOUND FROM MY MOUTH

Is a squashed tomato.

    The bullet races through my mind and spits out my thoughts onto the sidewalk.

I'M CROUCHING WITH MY SKULL PUNCTURED

Blood leaking from my ear. I listen to it. It sounds just like the sea.

I COLLAPSE INTO IT

The kid looks at me. He lifts his free hand and wipes some of my blood sprayed on his cheek. He looks at it on his fingertips.

    "Fuck," he says to himself.

    He wipes the blood on his shorts.

    "Fuck me that was awesome…!" he yells out into the night.

THE KID HOOTS WITH HIS CHEST FULL

Waving his gun into the moonlight.

HIS VOICE PULLS FARTHER AND FARTHER

He's moving away as he's cheering to himself.

THE WHOLE WORLD IS A PIECE OF PAPER BEING TORN IN HALF

"Fuuuucckkkkkkkkk thaaaatttttt wasssssss aweeeesssommmmmmeeeee…"

I AM VASKA

THERE IS A BOY WHO IS NOW A MAN
Sniff, sniff. He's lying on the sidewalk on Teutonia Avenue.

GET UP, MAN-BOY-FLOP
I nudge my nose at his fallen knees.

GET UP, GET UP
I plow my nose into his slumpy shoulder.

ARF ARF ARF
I say to him.

ARF ARF ARF
I say to the street.

ARF ARF ARF
I say to Mother Nature.

WHAT'S ALL THE NOISE?
Mother Nature says with a shifting in the blades of grass.

I AM VASKA
And this is a boy who is now a man, you remember.

NICKY, NICKY, NIKOLAI

She says, shaking her leaves. The wind loops under my belly.

ARE YOU ANGRY WITH HIM, MOTHER, SINCE YOU HAVE LET HIM BE FLOPPED?

I ask her.

VASKA, THIS IS NONE OF YOUR BUSINESS, GO ON, SHOO

She says with the moon.

"You're one nosey dog, aren't you?"

The moon glow shines on the white hairs of my fur.

PLEASE, HELP HIM UP

I say to her, even though I know it is not my place. I'm just a dog. A dog who goes on living. When all kinds of non-dogs die again and again. Sniff, sniff.

ARE YOU ASKING FOR A FAVOR?

She says with the moisture in the air. There is a dewdrop forming on my nose.

Arf, arf, arf.

OH, VASKA YOU OLD DOG, YOU GET TOO ATTACHED

She says with a line of ants crawling past my paws.

I BOW MY NOSE AT HIS LIMPY HAND

I start licking his palm.

ALL RIGHT, ALL RIGHT, ALL RIGHT
She says with three salt stars in the black sky.

I LET MY TONGUE HANG OUT AS I BREATHE
I watch his crooked body in full flop on the sidewalk. I breathe the way I want him to breathe with me.

FOOTSTEPS LIKE MY BREATH
Like my breath, like my breath, like my breath, the woman is walking.

I TURN MY NOSE TO HER AND MY TAIL WAGS
Hiya, Ma'am, Hiya, Hiya.

SHE RUNS HER FINGERS THROUGH THE FUR BETWEEN MY EARS
I close my eyes it feels so good, Oh thank you, thank you, ma'am.

GOOD BOY, VASKA, GOOD BOY
I follow how her lips move. My eyes feel dark and light at the same time.

SHE LEANS DOWN TO HIM
Nicky, Nicky, Nikolai…

GOOD BOY
I kneel down and put my head on my paws.

HIS EYES OPEN

Hiya, friend.

VASKA?

He wheezes.

HIYA, HIYA, IT'S ME

"Oh, Vaska, oh, Vaska."
   He's a little boy.
   He's a scared boy.
   He's a bad boy.
   I'm a good boy.

THE WOMAN HELPS HIM SIT UP

She puts his head on her shoulder. His head leaks onto the soft pink fur she's wearing.

   She opens his mouth with one hand then puts her fingers inside.

   "Well, well, well," she says to herself.

   She smudges her fingers inside his mouth.

   His eyes grow big.

   "Ouch," he says slowly.

   She pulls out a gold necklace.

   "Good boy," she tells him.

PLEASE, MAKE IT SO IT DOESN'T HURT MY FRIEND

I say to the ma'am.

DON'T WORRY, VASKA, YOU OLD BOY

I'm a good, old boy.

GET HIM OUT OF HERE
Mother Nature says with a cricket's chirp.

COME ON, THE MA'AM SAYS
She puts her hand into a brown-hide bag. It has a light thread going in and out at the edges. She reaches inside. She pulls out the thing and unfolds it. She taps inside to make a dome. She puts it on my friend's head.

It covers up the spots that hurt.

She lifts him up and flops his arm over her shoulder. She starts walking and he's stumbling along with her. Sometimes his feet drag and sometimes he uses them. I follow behind.

NORMALLY DOGS AREN'T ALLOWED INSIDE
But the ma'am says, Come on, Vaska, to me. I sit at his feet. I like it there.

My friend gets plates of food. He eats everything. It smells greasy, sugary, pickled, salted, cream-filled, citrusy, heavy, prickly, mushy.

He throws down pieces to me and I eat them up, Yum, thank you, thank you, friend!

The ma'am brings him something else. She opens it in his palm. Solid. Dark.

It smells like non-food.

She opens it, so there is a top and a bottom.

"Here," she says.

He stares inside of it.

"You love numbers, don't you?" she says.

He nods.

"Go on, press the numbers you love."

He lifts his finger and pushes inside the thing. It makes a beep. He lifts and brings it back down. Another beep. Then another. Beep. Beep. Beep. Beep. Beep. Beep. Beep.

He puts it to his ear. His breath is long and tense. Friend. Your smell is changing.

"*Privet*," he says to someone who is not here.

PRIVET

LOVE
It cannot rest. It wants out.

HATE
It wants trouble. It makes trouble.

A VOICE BETWEEN THE WALLS
I told you I'd suck you off when I got out, didn't I? Didn't I promise you that?

KNUCKLES ON THE DOOR
One-two.

KNOCK, KNOCK
"Who is it?"

I SAID, KNOCK, KNOCK
"WHO IS IT?"

IT'S NICKY!
"Nicky?"

NICKY WHO?
"Nicky, Nicky, the key!
 "The key to the door, Olga."

THE KEY
Around your neck.
   Privet.

I'M IN AMERICA NOW
   The laughter is sailing.
      The voice is assailing.
      Small crystals of dew in the corners of the ceiling.

THE SUN IS BRIGHT AND THICK AND YELLOW
I'm outside Angelina's apartment building. Which is my home. I
feel dry and awake in the sunlight.

MY ANGEL
I pull out the keychain from my pocket. I beep it past the front
door. I take the elevator up to the sixth floor.

I'M IN THE HALLWAY
There's our door. Where Angelina and I live. Together.

I TAKE OUT THE KEY
I put it in the lock. I twist.

THE LOCK
He says, "has changed." The man. Behind me.

HIS SKIN
It's flush and dark against his white polo. His head is shaved.
Clean, tan Dockers. Concise jaw. Full lips. Resemblances.

HE LOOKS SO MUCH LIKE HER WHEN HE'S WAITING
Focused and timeless.

CARLOS?
I stutter.

IT'S NOT THAT HE SCARES ME
It's the amplitude of his eyes.

HE CROSSES HIS ARMS
His biceps squish against his ribs. The muscles rippling beneath the taut skin there, arms like biblical valleys. He's watching me. His legs are firmly planted, but nothing of him is tense. He's got all the time in the world.

LOCKS CHANGE
He says, "when people change."

DO YOU WANT TO COME IN?
He sighs with a sigh that is undisputable.

TO SEE ANGELINA
I can't control the heat in my cheeks.

HE UNCROSSES HIS ARMS
"I can't."

BROTHER, SISTER
"I'm still in Afghanistan…"

I SQUINT AND SQUINT AND SQUINT

He points to my sternum.

"It doesn't burn?"

"What?" I ask.

"Your neck."

THE KEY CLICKS INSIDE THE LOCK

The door slides open.

The hallway is deserted.

HI, BABY

Angelina. Hair undone. Lips parted. Eyes flowing toward me.

SHE KISSES ME ON THE MOUTH

"How was work?"

I SMELL

I tell her that I need to take a shower.

OLGA

She touches my shoulder. I turn around.

"Look what I got…"

She points to a bowl of peas on the counter.

I reach my hand in and take one pea. I put it in my mouth. It's cold and hard and fresh.

I TAKE A SHOWER

It steams. I grip and extend my fingers in the hot water.

WITH MY HAIR STILL WET

I walk into the kitchen. Angelina is leaning over the stovetop. The pan is sizzling. On the table, the cutting board is laid out with a peeled onion cut in half. She turns around.

"Wanna help?" she says.

I DO

I want to help.

SHE SMILES

And smiles and smiles.

OR ELSE

I can't stop looking at her mouth.

OLGA?

"Olga..." she says, "Olga..."

YES, MY ANGEL

"Come over here and help me..."

SHE PUTS HER HAND TO MY CHEEK

The other slides down to the countertop. Her hand is reaching across the table to the cutting board.

HER FINGERS TOUCH IT

Curl around it. Bring it closer.

HERE

She says, sliding it toward me.

I TAKE THE KNIFE IN MY HAND
"Well…"

WELL
My thumb makes contact with my finger around the handle. I squeeze.

PURE AND SOUND
"Olga, what are you doing?!"

MY MOUTH IS POOLING WITH COLDNESS
Un, deux, trois.

IN THE BEGINNING
There was the word.

THE KITCHEN SHAKES
Fists pounding on the walls. All the walls. Pounding. Punching. Screaming, "WAKE UP, WAKE UP, WAKE UP!!!"

YES, YES, YES
It's not a flood.

MY VOICE
Frost against my teeth.

FOOTSTEPS
As soft as rain.

THE HANDLE OF THE KNIFE
Full stop.

TRUTH
The apartment is so quiet, it's no longer an apartment.
  The interval is so full, it's no longer an interval.
  The sea is so wide, it's no longer the sea.

THE WAVES
I don't want it to end, I don't want it to end,

ACKNOWLEDGMENTS

Angel of resurrection, I am in gratitude.

Thank you mom, dad, Valick.

Rick Kinner, Kaisa Kinnunen, Vanja Hedberg, Scott Cooper, Divya Bala, Carrie-Anne James, Ida Skovmand, Sarra Ryma, Laure Orset-Prelet, Lauren Elkin, Derek Ryan, Nadja Spiegelman, Amélie Rousseau, Rosa Rankin-Gee, Theodore Haber, Jayne Batzofin, Silke Schroeder and Dr. Claire Finney— your care and support are part of this book.

Can't thank my agents enough, Jane Finigan my ride-or-die advocate in Europe and David Forrer in North America.

A special thank you to Eliza, Eric, and everyone at Two Dollar Radio. You really get me. My cup runneth over.

Books too loud to Ignore

ALSO AVAILABLE Here are some other titles you might want to dig into.

VIRTUOSO *A NOVEL BY*
YELENA MOSKOVICH

....

* Swansea University Dylan Thomas Prize, longlist
* A BEST SMALL PRESS BOOK FROM 2020
—Mallory Smart, *Maudlin House*

....

"A hint of Lynch, a touch of Ferrante, the cruel absurdity of Antonin Artaud, the fierce candour of Anaïs Nin, the stylish languor of a Lana del Rey song... Moskovich writes sentences that lilt and slink, her plots developing as a slow seduction and then clouding like a smoke-filled room." —SHAHIDHA BARI, *THE GUARDIAN*

As Communism begins to crumble in Prague in the 1980s, Jana's unremarkable life becomes all at once remarkable when a precocious young girl named Zorka moves into the apartment building with her mother and sick father. With Zorka's signature two-finger salute and abrasive wit, she brings flair to the girls' days despite her mother's protestations to not "be weird." But after scorching her mother's prized fur coat and stealing from a nefarious teacher, Zorka suddenly disappears.

Meanwhile in Paris, Aimée de Saint-Pé married young to an older woman, Dominique, an actress whose star has crested and is in decline. A quixotic journey of self-discovery, *Virtuoso* follows Zorka as she comes of age in Prague, Wisconsin, and then Boston, amidst a backdrop of clothing logos, MTV, computer coders, and other outcast youth. But it isn't till a Parisian conference hall brimming with orthopedic mattresses and therapeutic appendages when Jana first encounters Aimée, their fates steering them both to a cryptic bar on the Rue de Prague, and, perhaps, to Zorka.

With a distinctive prose flair and spellbinding vision, *Virtuoso* is a story of love, loss, and self-discovery that heralds Yelena Moskovich as a brilliant and one-of-a-kind visionary.

Books to read!

Now available at **TWODOLLARRADIO.com** or your favorite bookseller.

NIGHT ROOMS ESSAYS GINA NUTT

⇥ "Together, these pieces form an experience that is sensory, intellectual and emotional, illuminating difficult and even uncomfortable truths." —Julia Kastner, *Shelf Awareness*

NIGHT ROOMS IS A POETIC, INTIMATE collection of personal essays that weaves together fragmented images from horror films and cultural tropes to meditate on anxiety and depression, suicide, body image, identity, grief, and survival.

THE HARE NOVEL MELANIE FINN

← "[A] brooding feminist thriller." —*New York Times*

← "Finn has a gift for weaving existential and political concerns through tautly paced prose." —Molly Young, *Vulture*

AN ASTOUNDING NEW LITERARY THRILLER from a celebrated author at the height of her storytelling prowess, *The Hare* bravely considers a woman's inherent sense of obligation—sexual and emotional—to the male hierarchy.

TWO DOLLAR RADIO GUIDE TO NAMING YOUR BABY

WITH ALL THE SWAGGER of the Palmyra Pumpkin Princess, the Two Dollar Radio Guide to Naming Your Baby will help you name your child by calling attention to those names you should probably definitely avoid. While we can't promise your child will be a success, we can provide you with the tools necessary to ensure your child will not be an epic failure.

TWO DOLLAR RADIO GUIDE TO VEGAN COOKING

← "This cookbook is imaginative and creative while also featuring accessible vegan recipes that are both healthy (mostly) and just super delicious all around. Two thumbs way up, and all of my other fingers as well, for this creative little cookbook." —Audrey Farnsworth, *Fodor's Travel*

WE ARE ALL EXPLORERS, vegan food explorers—join us on this culinary journey as we slay Vegan Hunger Demons.

A HISTORY OF MY BRIEF BODY
ESSAYS BY BILLY-RAY BELCOURT

⇥ Lambda Literary Award, Finalist.

← "Stunning... Happiness, this beautiful book says, is the ultimate act of resistance." —Michelle Hart, *O, The Oprah Magazine*

A BRAVE, RAW, AND fiercely intelligent collection of essays and vignettes on grief, colonial violence, joy, love, and queerness.

Thank you for supporting independent culture!
Feel good about yourself.

ALLIGATOR STORIES BY DIMA ALZAYAT

⇢ **PEN/Robert W. Bingham Award for Debut Short Story Collection, longlist.**
⇢ **Swansea University Dylan Thomas Prize 2021, shortlist.**

← "A stellar debut... Alzayat manages to execute a short but thoughtful meditation on the spectrum of race in America from Jackson's presidency to present." —Colin Groundwater, *GQ*

THE AWARD-WINNING STORIES in Dima Alzayat's collection are luminous and tender, rich and relatable, chronicling a sense of displacement through everyday scenarios.

WHITEOUT CONDITIONS NOVEL BY TARIQ SHAH

← "*Whiteout Conditions* is both disorienting and visceral, hilarious and heartbreaking." —Michael Welch, *Chicago Review of Books*

IN THE DEPTHS OF A BRUTAL Midwest winter, Ant rides with Vince through the falling snow to Ray's funeral, an event that has been accruing a sense of consequence. With a poet's sensibility, Shah navigates the murky responsibilities of adulthood, grief, toxic masculinity, and the tragedy of revenge in this haunting Midwestern noir.

SOME OF US ARE VERY HUNGRY NOW
ESSAYS BY ANDRE PERRY

⇢ **Best Books 2019: *Pop Matters***

← "A complete, deep, satisfying read." —Gabino Iglesias, NPR

ANDRE PERRY'S DEBUT COLLECTION of personal essays travels from Washington DC to Iowa City to Hong Kong in search of both individual and national identity while displaying tenderness and a disarming honesty.

SAVAGE GODS MEMOIR BY PAUL KINGSNORTH

⇢ **A Best Book of 2019 —*The Guardian***

← "[*Savage Gods* is] a wail sent up from the heart of one of the intractable problems of the human condition: real change comes only from crisis, and crisis always involves loss."
—Ellie Robins, *Los Angeles Review of Books*

SAVAGE GODS ASKS, can words ever paint the truth of the world—or are they part of the great lie which is killing it?

THE BOOK OF X NOVEL BY SARAH ROSE ETTER

⇢ **Winner of the 2019 Shirley Jackson Awards for Novel**
⇢ **A Best Book of 2019 —*Vulture, Entropy, Buzzfeed, Thrillist***

← "Etter brilliantly, viciously lays bare what it means to be a woman in the world." —Roxane Gay

A SURREAL EXPLORATION OF ONE WOMAN'S LIFE and death against a landscape of meat, office desks, and bad men.

Books to read!

Now available at **TWODOLLARRADIO.com** or your favorite bookseller.

TRIANGULUM NOVEL BY MASANDE NTSHANGA

→ **2020 Nomo Awards Shortlist**
→ **A Best Book of 2019** —*LitReactor, Entropy*

← "Magnificently disorienting and meticulously constructed."
—Tobias Carroll, Tor.com

AN AMBITIOUS, OFTEN PHILOSOPHICAL AND GENRE-BENDING NOVEL that covers a period of over 40 years in South Africa's recent past and near future.

THE WORD FOR WOMAN IS WILDERNESS
NOVEL BY ABI ANDREWS

← "Unlike any published work I have read, in ways that are beguiling, audacious…" —Sarah Moss, *The Guardian*

THIS IS A NEW KIND OF NATURE WRITING — one that crosses fiction with science writing and puts gender politics at the center of the landscape.

AWAY! AWAY! NOVEL BY JANA BEŇOVÁ
TRANSLATED BY JANET LIVINGSTONE

→ **Winner of the European Union Prize for Literature**

← "Beňová's short, fast novels are a revolution against normality. "
—Austrian Broadcasting Corporation, ORF

WITH MAGNETIC, SPARKLING PROSE, Beňová delivers a lively mosaic that ruminates on human relationships, our greatest fears and desires.

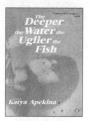

THE DEEPER THE WATER THE UGLIER THE FISH NOVEL BY KATYA APEKINA

→ **2018 *Los Angeles Times* Book Prize Finalist**
→ **A Best Book of 2018** —*Kirkus, BuzzFeed, Entropy, LitReactor, LitHub*
← "Nothing short of gorgeous." —Michael Schaub, NPR

POWERFULLY CAPTURES THE QUIET TORMENT of two sisters craving the attention of a parent they can't, and shouldn't, have to themselves.

THE BLURRY YEARS NOVEL BY ELEANOR KRISEMAN

→ **A Best Book of 2018** —*Entropy*
← "Kriseman's is a new voice to celebrate."—*Publishers Weekly*

THE BLURRY YEARS IS A POWERFUL and unorthodox coming-of-age story from an assured new literary voice, featuring a stirringly twisted mother-daughter relationship, set against the sleazy, vividly-drawn backdrop of late-seventies and early-eighties Florida.